Dancing the Salsa
By Raeshell Rozet

Dedicated to all who dream of trying something new.

Table of Contents

The Invitation 1

Chapter 1 Darkness, Darkness All Around me..............................5

Chapter 2 The Havana Night Club 10

Chapter 3 The Ride Home 16

Chapter 4 The Daily Grind 19

Chapter 5 Oxnard Bound...25

Chapter 6 La Pura Vida 29

Chapter 7 Dancing in Lompoc...39

Chapter 8 Dance with Me 51

Chapter 9 Meet Me in Havana 56

Chapter 10 La Purisma Mission 63

Chapter 11 So You Want to Dance?...73

Chapter 12 Esteban, The Dance Teacher..77

Chapter 13 Practice, Practice, Practice!...83

Chapter 14 Who Was That Guy?...85

Chapter 15 Did You Practice? 92

Chapter 16 The Cumbia King..96

Chapter 17 Don't You Dare Give Up 103

Chapter 18 A New Perspective...106

Chapter 19 Dancing on the Beach 120

Chapter 20 A Place of My Own 126

Chapter 21 Happy Thanksgiving...129

Chapter 22 Just the Two of Us 133

Chapter 23 Dancing with El Grupo 139

Chapter 24 The 805 144

Chapter 25 Breakfast at Midnight 154

Chapter 26 The Girl in the Mirror 157

Chapter 27 A New Opportunity..161

Chapter 28 It Begins 164

Chapter 29 LA Dreams...169

Chapter 30 The Grand Opening..171

Chapter 31 And the Show Goes On...181

Chapter 32 I've Had It 185

Chapter 33 An Unexpected Offer 189

Chapter 34 A Dream Come True...191

Chapter 35 Scrambled Eggs with Pablo 198
Chapter 36 Dancing is Better Than a Bag of Chips 205
Chapter 37 It's My Birthday...209
Chapter 38 Dancing with the Champions..221

The Invitation

"Another life whispers to me. And sometimes, the whispers become taps on my shoulder. It feels so close and I want it so much, but it remains thin as air. My own personal haunting. A ghost of another me telling me there is another way."

Until the ghost of myself made her presence known with those words in the beginning of the novel, I wasn't aware she had a part to play in the story, or that she even existed. But as the story continued on, she would present herself more and more. As she spoke up through my writing, I recognized her voice weaved through out the tale of my entire life.

Maybe you know this feeling I'm talking about? Something that lives just beyond your normal everyday life. Another you that exists only in your daydreams. That vision of something better that comes to you when your eyes are blurred with tears. That nagging thought if you just tried this one thing a whole new you might show up.

Scarlet is me, and her journey is more or less my life. Many of the events in the story happened, although some did not. All of the feelings, conflict, thoughts and voice of Scarlet is true to who I am, but this memoir is somewhat fictionalized as far as plot. The characters are not real, but rather composites made from numerous interactions and observations. Most of the material comes from my nights out dancing for almost a decade.

I tried to capture the beauty that I found in the music, the dancing and the people, but I confess words can only do so much. It's as if the first forty years of my life was a black and white movie, and then technicolor was invented. After tasting the richness and vitality of a colorful life, it saddens me to think of how dull my life could have been if it had remained in shades of grey.

Do you feel haunted by another life you're meant to have? If so, it is my sincerest hope that in each page of this book you'll feel my gentle encouragement. There is something more out there. Open yourself to the possibilities.

Chapter 1 Darkness, Darkness All Around me

Am I driving or am I driven?

Darkness, darkness all around me and every minute takes me farther away from my small town. Driving alone late at night is dangerous. I know that. Of course, I know that.

It's irresponsible. My two boys, Ben and Dan, are asleep at my mother's place. They are safe. But am I? This road is known for accidents. The dark and fog hide the twists and turns. A childhood friend was killed on this road by a drunk driver. She was decapitated. I'm fully aware of the risk. I feel a quiver in my hands as I grip the wheel.

My little Lompoc is far behind me, and Santa Barbara is about thirty minutes away. I'm halfway between the two worlds. The landscape changes from trees and hills to the ocean highway. The Pacific Ocean becomes my nighttime companion. It comforts me knowing she is there, but at the same time, her vastness magnifies my loneliness.

I wasn't always this way. For a long time, I tried to make my life as safe as possible. I was married with two boys, a dog, and a big blue house. I didn't drink or go to bars. Every night I stayed home. That was my life for twenty years.

And then it was gone. And I've been a little out of my mind ever since. Not crazy out of my mind, but my world has turned upside down and it seems the old rules of how to live life, gravity, and any other basic assumption I've ever had has been brought into question. I'm not sure of anything anymore.

Driving alone on this road, my mind travels back to the day my life unraveled. My husband, Gary, told me he was leaving. I loved him. I had tried my best to be a good wife and mother. I never cheated on him. I would have given up everything I had to keep my family together, but he wanted out.

What he said I can't repeat, not even to myself. The words, like a black magic, are too awful to conjure up. Gary knew exactly what to say to make me stop loving him instantaneously. It was as if he lifted a mask, and showed me his real face. I'd never be able to un-see it again. He drove off leaving me standing there speechless. The love was gone. One moment it was there, and the next obliterated. I wouldn't have believed that it was possible, but in an upside down world it can happen.

The truth is that we are all living in an upside down world. I think it is by grace that most people don't realize it. I don't have the heart to tell them. It can happen to anyone.

I follow the yellow line in the headlights which reveals just enough road to navigate the turns. The heat from the defroster keeps me warm even with my bare shoulders. Salsa music livens up the car. I don't understand many of the words, but my body knows the music. My eyes might watch the road ahead, but my mind sees dancing.

Another life whispers to me. And sometimes, the whispers become taps on the shoulder. It feels so close and I want it so much, but it remains thin as air. My own personal haunting. A ghost of another me telling me there is another way.

Or do I have it wrong? Am I the ghost chasing after her? Following by instinct, out into the middle of the night, away from my little town, searching for yet another clue as to how to become her. A ghost of myself wishing to become real.

I feel my car shudder as I go uphill. It rattles my nerves. Two hundred forty thousand. That's the number of miles on my car. I'm guessing that isn't good. It has been a faithful friend over the years, but I'm afraid I'm pushing it too hard in its old age. I know what I'm doing is not smart.

This is just one of many "not so smart" choices in my life. Getting married at the age of twenty-one. Choosing to be a stay at home mom. Trusting that my husband would stay by my side like I stayed by his during his career, which required us to move often. Sacrificing so we would have a decent retirement income in our golden years, which I lost the day he left me. I listen to my heart more than my head.

Living far away from home, I had no family or close friends around to help watch the kids. Teaching dance aerobic classes was the only job I found that worked with my children's school schedule. It's all I had to rebuild my life when my marriage fell apart. So when Gary left, I moved back in with my parents in Lompoc and started teaching dance aerobics in the gyms. Within four months, I had classes in all the gyms. In two of the facilities, I also work the front desk and as a Wellness Coach.

After the divorce, I lived my life as a shadow. I felt nothing. I barely slept. I had trouble keeping track of things. I don't even remember the exact date my divorce became final. My only goal was to get up each day to raise my kids and to help as many people as I could at the gyms.

For myself, I desired nothing, or maybe I felt like I deserved nothing. I doubt anyone would have guessed I felt this way. I hid it well. How could that Wellness Coach with a big smile on her face possibly be anything other than happy?

Something changed when I heard Lompoc was having its first Salsa Night. I felt something stir inside. Lompoc has little entertainment. The restaurants close at nine, and the streets are quiet. There are a couple of bars that stay open for drinking. That's it. No variety. This was different. It was like a breath of fresh air.

Although the Salsa Night happened four days ago, as I'm driving the coastal highway my mind replays it like a movie. A local restaurant, La Casa Roja, transformed itself into a Salsa Club for one night. It pushed back its tables for a dance floor, hired a deejay with fancy lights, and even splurged on a Salsa Instructor.

When the lesson began, men were instructed to stand in one line, and the ladies lined up facing them. The teacher demonstrated a pattern and then we practiced. When the teacher called out "Rotate" the women would move on to the next guy in the line.

I danced with several partners. Each one was polite and well-dressed, but none knew how to dance. I was launched across the dance floor and whipped into spins. Seeing that I was a beginner too, I was wobbly on my feet.

That's when I met Esteban Vazquez.

He had black hair with a few silver strands peppering the sides and deep brown eyes that I had a hard time looking into without shying away. His clothes fit nicely on his trim build. His light blue long sleeve shirt was the perfect color against his dark skin. He seemed reserved, a quiet person, and yet his smile said that he was friendly. Next to his smile, I saw a beauty mark on his right cheek. Placing my hands into his I knew there was something different about him. The feeling was so strong the teacher read my thoughts. I heard her say "This is good. You look good together" as she walked past us. It sounded like an odd thing to say, but it gave voice to what I was thinking.

The way he held my hands was new to me. He wasn't overpowering me by gripping them tightly, but I could feel his hands clearly guiding me, telling me when to move and when to stop. If I became confused, his hands directed me the right way, gained my balance after a spin, or even protected me from other dancers who were dancing too close. He didn't say anything except to introduce himself, and our parting was a gentle hug that I gave him with a "Thank you" when the teacher said "Rotate."

I danced with him off and on throughout the night. We didn't talk much. He would walk over to me, extend a hand, and out we would go on to the dance floor.

Each dance was a thrill ride with unexpected twists and spins. The music carried happiness and a promise that for now at least, life feels good. The lights were flashing colors of red, blue, green, white, and purple as I spun around Esteban. I had no idea what I was doing, but he guided me and kept me safe. The feel of his hands, the smell of his cologne, I took everything in. I could feel myself smiling, and even when I tried, I couldn't stop.

I asked the instructor about Esteban. She said that he had come up from Oxnard to help her out. He's a dance teacher, and she knows him from dancing in the clubs in Santa Barbara and Oxnard.

I hoped he would ask for my phone number, but he never did. After the night finished, I was left with the memory of feeling alive when I danced. I was no longer a shadow.

That's why I called my friend Cindy. She lives in Santa Barbara. She invited me out to the Salsa clubs when I first moved back to Lompoc, but I wasn't ready. This afternoon I tried my luck and sent a text to see when we could hit a club. She said one was happening tonight, and told me to meet her at the Havana Night Club.

I don't know what to expect. I barely know how to dance with a partner. I'm a nightmare at spinning. I get dizzy. And dips? Nope. I have the least flexible body ever made for a woman. This could be really bad. But, none of those things matter to me. I keep listening to the Salsa music playing in the car, and I see myself dancing.

Chapter 2 The Havana Night Club

I hear the music even from the parking lot. People are still walking into the club at eleven. I hop out of my car and follow the crowd. Like a child lured by the Pied Piper, the music draws me inside.

Luckily, it only costs five bucks to get in. Straight ahead, I see the bar which reaches across the length of the room. To my left, the dance floor is only a few feet away with bright lights and spinning girls. They make it look easy. How do the girls know what to do? They add in clever hair tosses, body rolls, and hold both hands over their head as they spin. I feel nervous. There's no way I can dance like that.

"Hey there!" I hear as Cindy gives me a hug. "You made it!"

"I did," I tell her as I hug her back. I'm about to say more when the deejay comes up to us. He has blonde hair and green eyes with a few freckles on his cheeks. I'm guessing he's in his late twenties.

He gives Cindy a hug and a kiss on the cheek. She introduces us and before I know what's happening, he's leading me onto the dance floor.

"Wait!" I hear Cindy call out trying to stop him, but it's too late.

The music is too loud for me to say anything like "I don't know how to dance", "I've only had one lesson" or "please don't dip me because I haven't figured out how to do that yet."

I wish I could say that I mystically knew what to do and did it beautifully. No such luck. He tried to spin me out onto the dance floor, and it made me dizzy. He tried to do the Salsa basic, a simple forward-together-back-together movement, and I kept losing the beat. I froze. His face looked as confused as mine. Thank God, he didn't try to dip me. We ended up doing the basic step for pretty much the whole song. It was awful. He was very sweet. He thanked me for the dance, gave me a kiss on the cheek, and escorted me back to Cindy.

She felt bad for me.

"I tried to stop him."

"I know you did."

"He thought you could dance because you were with me."

"That's okay," I tell her, and it really is okay. I want to learn how to dance. Humiliation is a small price to pay.

Cindy carefully arranges my next dance. She introduces me to Rick.

"Rick, this is my friend, Scarlet Stevens. She is just learning how to dance. This is her first time at the club."

"Hello, Scarlet."

"Hi, Rick. Nice to meet you," I answer as he shakes my hand.

"Would you like to dance?"

"Yes, but I don't know how to very well. I've only had one lesson. I'm not good at spinning," I try to give a detailed warning label as we walk onto the dance floor.

"That's all right. We were all beginners once."

His words put me at ease. It's the sound of his voice. There is a calmness to it. It makes me feel like I can do nothing wrong. My shoulders relax.

He also has an uncanny resemblance of my father's face or the face of my father when he was younger. My dad has Scottish blood, and there is a squareness of his chin and eyes that I see in Rick. It is a quality I find from time to time in men that I can't put into words. It's either there or not.

Rick is easy to follow. Gently, he leads my right hand back which naturally makes me step back with my right foot on the first beat, then he guides my left hand forward on the fifth beat which signals me to step forward with my left foot, and just like that I can keep time with him on the Salsa basic.

He's tall. So whenever I look up at him I see this big smile shining down on me. He lifts my right hand to signal a turn. I spin around and get myself dizzy as usual, but he shines me that grin and puts me at ease. Even if it isn't perfect, I'm having fun. Somehow he knows how to place me wherever I need to be, whether it's walking across him to the other side or staying in place while he spins.

I let the music pass through me, and I get myself lost in it. The lights, the crowded dance floor, my partner and the feeling of myself having a place in it all. When the song ends, Rick takes me back to Cindy.

She's smiling, and already has guy number three lined up and ready to go. Soon after, I have no problem finding Salseros willing to take me on the dance floor. I suspect most of the men have already had a chance to see that I am a beginner, so fortunately I haven't found anyone with high expectations.

I've already started to form my own dance rules. Never turn anyone down, unless they are drunk. A song only lasts a few minutes, and It takes courage to ask someone out on the dance floor, so why be rude? Try to avoid dancing three songs in a row with the same guy. The first dance is fun, the second starts to feel clingy, and by the third I feel trapped. I have no idea why I feel this way. I just do. No matter what, bad smells, strange quirks, stepped on foot, try to smile. From what I can see, the Salsa world is small. Everyone knows everyone. It's best to be forgiving.

There is no concept of time on the dance floor. The music creates its own current and once you're lost swimming in it you just keep going until you're covered in sweat and out of breath. The Havana Night Club has an outside patio that you can escape to from the dance area.

The cool air is fresh against my skin. The open sky is clear with stars. I see a couple of planes moving along in an otherwise still world. It's pretty out here. To my left is an outside fireplace providing a source of natural heat and light. Along one side of the perimeter there is a seating area with a whitewashed wooden covering adorned with plants that drape down. The setting is perfected with table candles giving a soft glow. But what catches my eye is Cindy dancing in the middle of the miniature courtyard with a handsome man.

It's simply beautiful. Cindy has dancer lines. She stands tall. Her movements are disciplined, but fluid. There is an air of spontaneity and wild abandonment that is exciting and keeps me watching. Her long dark hair is pulled back into a ponytail which complements her long split skirt and heels. Her eyes gaze into her partner's, and when she spins her eyes return to him even before her body.

Her partner is equally skilled. He orchestrates their movements to naturally flow with the music. He pauses to give Cindy opportunities to shine and style, and adds his own footwork without losing the connection to lead. He is an older gentleman. I'm guessing in his fifties by the touch of grey on his black hair, but on the dance floor he looks ageless. It's as if dancing turns back the hands of time, if only for a song.

He wears a light grey suit with a white shirt that favors his olive skin tone and trim build. He pays attention to details down to his polished shoes and the way he executes his movements. He smiles at Cindy as if she is the most beautiful woman in the room.

I'm not the only one watching. The young couple standing by the fire. The group of friends drinking at the table. We watch as Cindy spins towards the man. He catches her lowering her into a dip and then quickly lifts her up to be embraced in his arms. They slowly part into holding hands again. The song ends, and they part ways.

Cindy walks towards me.

"That was so beautiful. How do you do it?"

"Practice, a lot of practice," she laughs.

"I can't even spin or figure out what the guy wants me to do."

"You should try to get to the club early. They give a free lesson before the dancing starts."

"I wish I could, but I work at the gym until nine. I can't get here any earlier. Do you take lessons?" I ask.

"I used to be part of a dance team back when I lived in San Francisco. I still try to arrange for a private lesson with my teacher whenever I can make it over that way, which is probably once every other month or so."

"You drive all the way to San Francisco for lessons?" I figure that's about a seven-hour drive from Santa Barbara.

"Yes, I've been doing that for a few years now."

"And you go out dancing during the week?"

"Yes, I go dancing about three nights a week."

"How do you do it? Don't you get tired?"

"No, I just love it."

There is no way I could do that, not with my kids still living at home. But I know Cindy doesn't have children, and she's not married.

"Do you have a boyfriend?"

"Sometimes," she smiles and adds, "but never anyone from Salsa."

I'm about to ask why when another guy approaches and asks her out onto the dance floor.

Chapter 3 The Ride Home

On my long drive home, I playback the night in my head. It's two o'clock in the morning, but I'm not tired. The Santa Barbara city lights are behind me, and the ocean is to my left. Salsa music floats my mind back to the club. I danced with so many men, but I can barely recall their faces. One just blends into the next.

To me, it's all about the dancing. The men are interchangeable. I could care less if they are handsome or homely, skinny or fat, tall or short, green or purple. I'm sure some of the men I danced with tonight would make my friends back in Lompoc green with envy, but if one walked up to me tomorrow I doubt I'd recognize him. Everything is in the moment, and when the moment is gone, so is his face.

I didn't see Esteban. The thought hadn't crossed my mind until now. There was a part of me hoping I'd run into him, but I had no such luck. His face I remember.

The sign ahead reads "Mariposa Reina" and out of nowhere I have an overwhelming sense of being surrounded by nothingness. It strikes me that I really am out here alone and that I shouldn't be. Maybe it's more than just being by myself on the road? It's the realization that my husband has left me, and I'm alone in the world. The aloneness that hits you in the stomach and the soul.

I focus on the Salsa song playing to settle my nerves. Images of the last dance of the night come to me like an instant replay. My partner was younger than me, but that didn't seem to bother him. I can't pull together enough details of his face to create a mental picture, but I do remember he had deep brown eyes and a kind grin. I'm sure he told me his name, but again, I'm drawing a blank.

He shook his shoulders. I shook mine. He moved across me and somehow I moved across him to the other side too. Remembering the laughing and smiling during the dance, I feel myself smiling as I'm driving home in the car.

If it wasn't for dancing, I don't think my sons would ever see me smile. They would only see me miserable and sad. Hope is one of the things I'm searching for, and the legacy I want to give my boys. Things will get better. Life won't always feel this bad.

When the unthinkable, unimaginable, or unfathomable happens in an upside down world, I want my boys to know they can find a way to stand, and while standing, smile again.

Yes, I guess anything is possible in an upside down world, even good things when you would expect only sadness.

The tunnel is up ahead. It is the dividing point between the Ocean highway and the more dangerous part of the drive. What makes the road dangerous is the combination of drunk drivers, unexpected bends in the road, pockets of fog, and those who speed and lose control of their vehicle. Also, wildlife that come out of nowhere. I once had a group of seven black wild pigs run across the road. Growing up local and hearing countless stories of unfortunate accidents, I'm a careful driver. I respect this road.

Again, to distract myself from the heebie-jeebies, I think about my talk with Cindy as we left the club. The last song had ended, and the houselights turned on to signal it was time to go home. I couldn't believe it was over. It went by so fast. Cindy and I walked out to the parking lot together.

"Did you like it?" She asked.

"I loved it. Thanks for meeting me here. I wouldn't have known about this place if it wasn't for you."

"You're welcome. Are you going to be okay driving home? You can stay at my place."

"Thanks, but I have to wake up early to get my son to school, and I teach an aerobics class at eight-thirty."

"All right, but the offer stands if you decide you need to. I must admit you're braver than me. As much as I love dancing, driving alone at night gives me the creeps."

"I had so much fun. It was worth it. Are you coming here next week?"

"Yeah, this is one of my regular dance places. I come every week. Why? Are you coming back?"

"Yes, definitely."

"You're hooked. I'll see you next Thursday then. Drive safe," she gave me a big hug.

The hug felt good even though I worried she'd feel that I was soaked with sweat. And just like that, I set myself up with a place to dance every week.

I'm down to the last turn of my drive. I see the Lompoc city lights emerge out of the darkness, and I know I've made it home safely. I love those lights. I breathe easier. The Salsa music keeps playing until the car stops at the house, and then it continues on in my dreams and in my heart.

Chapter 4 The Daily Grind

"I love you, kiddo. Have a great day at school."

"Love you too, Mom."

Dan enters the school gate and crosses the field to his second grade classroom. I'm completely broken. How could his father do this? What must my son be feeling? My father left too, but I was a little older, fourteen. I remember my dad telling me that one day, when I became an adult, I would understand. But the older I got, the only thing I understood was just how wrong he was to leave his family. It kills me that I can do nothing to prevent my son from being hurt. Watching him through the fence is like watching my heart with child-like legs, vulnerable and exposed, walk away from me. I feel helpless.

My real legs feel like lead, but I have to rush to make it to my Latin aerobics dance class which starts in twenty minutes. Then I have to teach another dance class at a military base gym, and after race back to town to work as a Wellness Coach at Women4Fitness. Around dinner time, I will end the evening working the front desk at the Lompoc Valley Gym until closing.

I don't trust my brain this morning, so I've been double checking myself making sure I have everything packed (change of clothes, music, lunch). Functioning on less than three hours of sleep, I am determined that staying out all night won't affect my work.

I love teaching Latin dance aerobics. The Latin rhythms rush through my veins inducing the hallucination that life can only feel good. It's rare for me to miss a class. You never know who might need it that day. I remember the first time I had someone approach me after class to confide in me. Her name was Eleanor. She was a sweet woman who regularly attended class twice a week. Her mother had just passed away.

"I want to thank you," Eleanor began when we were alone in the room. "You don't know this, but your class really helped me while I was taking care of my mother. It was so hard to watch her wasting away, and the one thing that kept me going was knowing that I could come to your class."

Eleanor didn't share her struggle with any of us. I had no idea she was suffering. All I could recall was seeing her smile and laugh while she danced. The first one to share a joke or offer encouragement to someone new. That's when I realized I wasn't the only one who used exercise for survival on bad days. She and I are kindred spirits.

Since then I've had at least a dozen share similar experiences. The circumstances are different, but the underlining theme of pain relief echoes in each sharing. My guess is that there are many more that suffer in silence that I will never know about. This is the one place where we can feel good for an hour, laugh, smile, and talk to friends. When it is over and life resumes, the memory will be a reminder in dark hours that there will be another opportunity to feel good again.

The adrenaline from the dance aerobics classes keeps me going for most of the day, but by mid-afternoon I'm feeling the heaviness come back in my legs. I'm waiting in the lobby of Women4Ftiness for my Get Fit appointment to arrive.

I see a woman with light brown hair and glasses walk towards the front desk. She's wearing black yoga pants, a large faded pink sweatshirt, and brand new tennis shoes. She's thirty-pounds overweight and looks uncomfortable being here. I'm guessing she's my three o'clock appointment.

"Hi, I'm Scarlet. Is your name Mary?"

"Yes," she shakes my hand.

"I'm so glad to meet you. I'm the Wellness Coach for your Get Fit appointment. We can talk in the office or if you prefer we can sit outside since the weather is nice."

"I'd like to sit outside and talk," Mary gives a smile.

I lead her outside to a bench under a tree. I find a lot of newcomers feel more relaxed talking outside. They get to know me a little bit. Hopefully, I make them laugh at least once during the conversation. When we finally enter the gym for the workout, they feel like they've already made a friend.

"I have to confess I prefer having these appointments outside. The weather is usually beautiful. Before we start working on a fitness plan, I'd like to get to know you. I like to tailor the workouts to fit your needs. What are your goals?"

She looks down at her hands. Mary's smile disappears.

"I've been through a rough time. I've divorced my husband," Mary pauses before starting again. Staring at her hands as though they'll give her extra strength, she continues, "He used to abuse me."

I watch her eyes tear up, but I stay silent. I let her take her time sharing.

"I have three kids, and I want to be strong for them. I want a better life for all of us," she finally looks up at me. I remain quiet to let her speak.

"I'm overweight, and my doctor says I'm pre-diabetic. My parents both had diabetes, and I don't want to be like them. My kids need me, so I have to take care of myself. I'm determined."

"We're going to come up with a plan to make this happen," I choose my words carefully. Who knows? I may be the only person in her life telling her she can do this.

"Are you currently working out?" I ask.

"I've started walking three days a week for about half an hour."

"That's great! Walking is a good start. How long have you been doing this?

"For about a month."

"Perfect. I like that you've already started getting in the habit of moving regularly. How many days a week can you make it to the gym?"

"I can definitely make it three days a week, possibly four, but I'm not sure about that."

"To start with we're going to commit to three days a week. If you make it that extra day you're going to give yourself a pat on the back, okay?"

She is smiling again. I've taken the pressure off her. She knows I'm not going to make this impossible. My goal is to give her something she can succeed at and build on. I'll ask about her health history, eating habits, and start showing her the machines in the gym. I'll come up with a plan to get her started and book the next appointment, but what really matters is the bond we are forming. She has trusted me with what she wants most, and I am now her partner in making her dream a reality.

And at four o'clock, I will start the process over again with another person with a new goal. That's how I spend every hour at Women4Fitness. I'm usually booked. Sometimes people have to wait a week or two for an appointment. Just another reason why staying out all night cannot affect my work.

By the time the big clock on the wall says it's eight, I'm dead tired. I'm down to my last hour at my last job. Luckily, the Lompoc Valley gym is quiet tonight. From the front desk, I count only five people in the workout area.

"So, how was the Salsa dancing?" Mike's giving me one of his drop dead smiles as he approaches. With his perfect body and easy going manner, he is a favorite among the female members of the gym.

"I loved it. I had so much fun. But, I'm terrible at it."

"I don't believe you. I've seen you teach your classes."

"It's completely different. My classes are planned and practiced. Dancing with a partner leading means I'm reacting to everything. I can't spin to save my life. I get dizzy and lose my balance."

Mike just shakes his head and smiles. I don't know if he believes me or not. He's five years older than me, and still handsome. He has dark hair with green eyes and is at least six feet tall. I've had a lot of women approach me to find out if he's available. The truth is I don't know. I've never asked.

What I like about Mike is the way he makes me feel. His favorite way to great me? "Here she comes, the Amazing Scarlet!" I love hearing that although it embarrasses me every time.

"I'm sure you danced with a lot of guys."

"Yeah, but I didn't know what I was doing."

"Are you going to try it again?"

"Of course, same time, same place, next week."

"Scarlet, the Amazing Salsa Dancer," he proclaims as he walks away to finish his workout.

Mike is my co-worker. He teaches a boot camp class. He knows I'm studying to become a Personal Trainer. His encouragement helps whenever I doubt myself.

The gym closes, and I finally go home. I'm grateful to be living with my parents. Without their help picking up my sons from school and feeding them dinner I don't know how I'd be able to work these hours. Plus, I know my kids are around family that loves them like I do, and that my parents and I share the same values.

I talk to my boys about their day. Dan, the second-grader, shares stories about recess and friends. Ben, a senior in high school, talks about band practice and Physics class.

As I watch my sons, I see both my ex-husband and myself blended in each of them. Both boys have blonde hair like their father, but instead of being straight like his they have a slight wave from me. Ben has my olive skin tone and a tall, lanky build like his dad. Dan is the opposite having lean muscle like me, but favoring his father's fair skin. When my sons look at me, I see their father's blue eyes, strong and confident. But their smiles, definitely take after mine. No matter how awful I feel about the divorce, I could never see the marriage as a mistake. How could I? My sons are so incredibly beautiful.

When I enter my bedroom, my legs are beyond tired. My eyes are red. I crawl into bed. My body may be wrecked, but my soul is happy. I have something to think about other than what a mess my life has turned out to be.

Ever since my husband left I experience these strange episodes of waking up in the middle of the night with no memory of the divorce. I slowly come to the awareness that my husband isn't lying beside me. I remember I am alone. I'm at my parents' house. Details of the divorce start to come back to me. Nothing around me feels real. And finally, I realize that this is my life. When I go through this it's scary as hell, so I dread going to sleep.

Tonight is different. I want to fall asleep. I'm exhausted. If I have to go through that terrible ordeal of remembering the divorce again, memory by painful memory, I know in the end my mind will think of dancing. And when I think of dancing, I always smile. I can't help myself. I just do.

Chapter 5 Oxnard Bound

I'm on the road again. It's Saturday, my day off from work. This time I'm heading out earlier. Tonight, I have farther to travel. My boys are visiting their father this weekend, so there's no reason for me to stay home. Cindy has invited me to go with her to a Salsa club in Oxnard called La Pura Vida. I'm picking her up in Santa Barbara. We'll make the rest of the drive together.

The road seems less treacherous at seven o'clock than it does at ten. It could be I feel more at ease, because I know I don't have to make the long drive home tonight. I'm going to crash at Cindy's place.

I'm excited to try a club in Oxnard. Cindy tells me that I will probably see a lot of familiar faces from the Havana Club, because most dancers in this area frequent the clubs in Santa Barbara, Oxnard, and LA. And yeah, I haven't forgotten that Esteban lives in Oxnard. I've yet to see him in Santa Barbara. Maybe tonight I might run into him.

Salsa music makes the drive pass quickly. Before long, I'm knocking on Cindy's apartment door.

"Hello. Come inside," she gives me a big hug.

I love Cindy's place. The words "classy and comfortable" spring to mind. It's a white space with accents of light-colored wood and green plants. There's a seamless coordination of elements that produces a visual peace. Her home matches her dancing style, the combination of elegant and natural.

"I'm still getting ready. I keep changing my mind about what to wear. Can you help me decide?"

What I see surprises me. Her bed is a mess. There are at least a dozen failed attempts for a potential Salsa outfit lying dead on the bed. Each one is gorgeous, but rejected like a jilted beauty pageant runner up.

"Are you ready for tonight?" Cindy asks as she puts together another ensemble. She slips on a red dress that hugs her body closely, highlighting her tiny waist and perfect curves.

"You have to wear that one. The men are going to go crazy."

"Yeah, this dress fits my mood. I'll wear it." Cindy takes a long look at my clothes.

"I have something I want you to try on." She hands me an itty bitty black dress with spaghetti straps.

I'm doubtful. I exercise a lot, but this dress is going to be unforgiving of any imperfections. Still, I manage to squeeze into it.

Cindy is smiling.

"You look beautiful."

I see myself in the mirror. I've never seen myself this way before. The dark color brings out my light brown eyes. The tiny dress shows off my skin which is a light olive tone from my mix of Scottish, German, and Filipino ancestry. My dark brown hair falls past the spaghetti straps to the middle of my back. The black dress shows off my legs which are nicely sculpted from all the aerobics classes I teach. Since I always wear sneakers instead of heels I had no idea that my calves had such definition. The dress has two small triangular strips of sheer black fabric on each side of my waist to allow my abs to show through. Instead of being trashy its done in such a subtle way that I like it.

"You don't mind if I use it?"

"Not at all. Now that you're dancing Salsa, we'll have to work on your wardrobe. This is a good start, although the skirt could be shorter."

"No, I don't think so."

Cindy laughs, "You'll be surprised what you'll think in a year or two. Here. You need to wear this underneath." She hands me a pair of small black spandex shorts. "From now on, you need to wear shorts under your dress when you dance. Then you don't have to worry when the guy dips you or flips you."

"Flip?"

She laughs again. "The guys only do it with the girls they know can handle it. You should consider buying dance shoes too. Here, let me show you." She pulls out a pretty black high heel shoe from her closet and turns it over so I can see the bottom portion where the shoe makes contact with the floor. "See, this is suede. It allows you to spin without too much friction, but it has just enough hold so you don't slide all over the place either."

"I need all the help I can get with spinning. Thanks for showing me. I'll have to buy a pair. And by the way, thanks for introducing me to the clubs and your friends. It really means a lot."

"No worries. I love introducing people to Salsa. And you know, I went through a divorce too."

"Really? I had no idea. When?"

"About five years ago. It hurt like hell," after a pause and a breath she continued, "I think Salsa is going to be good for you. It helps. When you get divorced you feel lonely. You want to be around people, but at the same time, you don't want anyone to ask about your life. Their lives seem so normal, and yours feels so messed up. Dancing is a way to be around people without having to talk or explain anything. You can just have fun."

"That's exactly how I feel. To be honest, I'm so focused on learning how to dance I can't even remember most of the men I've danced with. I couldn't care less what they look like. I just want to dance."

"I get it. But you know, the human contact is a good thing, even the holding of the hands or smiling at your partner. I think that's why I haven't had a boyfriend for a while. I don't really need one. It's hard to feel lonely when you dance with so many men," Cindy looks me in the eye and gives a sly grin. Is it because she knows I feel the same way or is she trying to give me helpful advice?

I just laugh. Her words make sense to me.

Chapter 6 La Pura Vida

We pull into the parking lot of La Pura Vida. The place is not what I expected. Whereas the Havana Night Club is more upscale with its freshly painted walls, miniature courtyard and fireplace, La Pura Vida has no such fancy dressing. The club is plunked in the corner of a shopping center next to a laundromat. The Latin rhythms are calling out to us in the parking lot and blinking colored lights of gold, blue and red dance through the open front door and window glass.

People trickle into the club. Some are dressed up and others are wearing jeans and t-shirts. La Pura Vida welcomes all types.

A man at the front door collects our five dollars. I love that these clubs only charge five bucks. Since I don't drink this makes it a cheaper night out than a movie. The layout is simple. To the left is a bar that travels the wall with bar stools filled with people (mostly men). To the right, I see a stage where the deejay does his magic. In front of the stage, there is a large rectangular dance floor bordered by tables and chairs on each of its sides. No one can get lost. It isn't as glamorous and seductive as the Havana Club, but I like the openness and informality. It's friendly and inviting.

Cindy leads the way to our table. She gives a hug and kiss to at least ten people as we move through the club, taking the time to introduce me to each one before we finally sit down.

"Hey Cindy," a blonde-haired girl in a red silk sleeveless top and blue jeans walks up to us.

"Hi Maria, come sit with us. I want you to meet my friend, Scarlet. She's come all the way from Lompoc."

"Hi, Maria. Nice to meet you," I say as I stand up to give her a hug.

"Nice to meet you too. You came from Lompoc? Where is that?"

"It's about an hour north of Santa Barbara. It's a small town."

"That's a long way to drive!"

"Yeah, I know, but it's worth it. There's not much Salsa dancing in Lompoc."

She starts to sit down, but a guy comes by and asks her to dance. And just like that, she's whisked off to the dance floor.

Her dance style is different from Cindy's. Her moves are unrefined. I can tell she hasn't been dancing as long. Still, she has her own flair. There is a natural, earthiness to her movements, and her steps are on the beat. Her signature move is the toss of her long blonde hair after a spin. It is stunning.

"Do you see how she dances?" Cindy asks.

"Yes, she has her own style. I like it."

"Maria hasn't been dancing very long, but she's a natural. What she lacks in technique she makes up with her own flavor. Plus, she has an outgoing personality, and it shows when she dances."

"I can see that."

"You can do that too. Even if you don't know a lot about Salsa, you are a sweet person and easy to talk to. You can use that when you dance with people. Try to find your own style and just be yourself," as she finishes her advice a guy comes up to our table, extends his hand to Cindy, and she is gone.

I'm sitting at the table alone. This feels awkward. Still, it does give me the opportunity to watch how people dance. It's early so the dance floor isn't crowded.

My eye catches a couple dancing close to me. It looks like they're engaged in a battle of the wills. They are both polite and smiling, but you can see their mutual frustration. The guy is offbeat. I'm guessing he doesn't know this by the way he insists his partner follow. To her credit, she's trying to follow, but seems unsure which beat he is dancing to. I hold back a laugh, because at one point I see her trying to watch his feet in a desperate attempt to figure out what music he's following in his head. Nothing seems to help, because the guy doesn't seem to be dancing to any predictable musical pattern. He is now giving her verbal directions by counting for her out loud. The sad part is that if I'm lip reading correctly his counting makes no sense at all. My eyes leave them as they struggle along to finish the song.

My attention turns to an older couple dancing in the center of the floor. Both have some gray in the hair and extra padding in the mid-section. The woman is wearing a flower print dress with red heels. Her partner is in slacks and a long sleeved dress shirt. They communicate effectively with one another, each one reading the other well so that their movements are coordinated. The guy seems to keep recycling the same seven combinations, but neither one looks bored. Instead, the two smile at one another and give their all. I wouldn't be surprised to find out that they're married and have been dancing the same steps for years.

Not far from them, I see a woman hanging on for dear life. She looks like she bought a ticket for a rollercoaster ride she regrets. I don't think she's been dancing long. She looks unsteady on her feet, but that doesn't stop the spins from coming. Her partner looks like he has a plan, and he's going to stick to it. He seems oblivious to his follower's distress. Her undone hair, stumbling footwork, and straight-lined mouth. If she falls, I think the man will continue to drag her body along until the song is done.

Dancing in front of the bar area, I see a man in a white Fedora hat dipping a woman in silver heels. This couple is dancing for the crowd. They want to be seen, and everyone at the bar is watching them. Their movements are more intricate and complex than the rest of the dancers. It looks more like a choreographed routine rather than a spontaneous flowing dance. The woman stretches her right arm overhead and extends her fingers with her middle finger and thumb spaced as if they were holding a deck of cards and the rest of the fingers spread like a fan, and then carefully traces her hand behind her head and down the length of her side while spinning. The man's footwork is complicated adding extra steps and accents. The moves are exciting, but I daresay it borders on almost overdone. Unlike the older couple, I doubt they are in love. Their enjoyment seems to come from the attention of the onlookers rather than each other. I suspect they are partners of sorts, dance instructors, and this is part of their business.

My trance is interrupted by a man dressed in white. He is wearing white shiny shoes, white pants and a white short-sleeved shirt. He asks me for a dance. I place my hand in his and he leads me onto the dance floor.

The music has changed to a Bachata. These songs are usually slower than Salsa, and most would say sexier. The couples dance close together. They use more body rolls, head rolls, and slow dips. Instead of moving forward and back, the Bachata basic is three steps to the right with a tap, and three steps to the left with a tap. Part of the sensuality of the dance is that the woman accentuates the tap with a lift of her hip giving Bachata its flavor.

My partner is easy to follow. I like that he has a smooth style that matches the mood of the song. He repeats the same pattern of steps so I'm able to predict what comes next. In Bachata, I spin as I travel to one side which gives me three steps to complete the turn and makes it easier than in Salsa. Unfortunately, I still get dizzy.

He has an intense stare. I can't quite read it. I'm more focused with the fact that I am starting to learn how to dance. He pulls me forward for three steps and then back for three. Each time we move backwards he leans into me more. We switch to the side steps again and when he lifts his hand I turn. He doesn't smile. Since the steps are predictable, I'm starting to figure out how to lift my hip with each tap. I'm experimenting with it.

The song ends, but he doesn't let me go. He keeps dancing with me as the next Bachata song starts to play. Since I'm starting to figure out the steps I don't try to pull away. The dance floor is getting crowded now. I have people close to me on all sides. He does some kind of rock step and then he brings me across him to the other side. I've figured out the footwork, and I'm playing with adding an extra hip movement. I almost have something that works with the timing. I'm concentrating so intently I barely notice that the song has changed. Again, he doesn't want to let go of my hands.

That's it for me. I break the connection and thank him for the dance.

My friends are waiting for me at the table.

"I think you have an admirer," Maria tells me as I sit down. "He's still watching you."

"I don't like him," Cindy adds. "There's something about the way he looked at you when you danced. It gave me the creeps."

"Well, creepy or not, he is handsome," Maria nudges me and smiles.

"I don't know. I just don't have a good feel about him. I haven't seen him around before. He must be new," Cindy says as a guy leads her away to dance again.

"Do you like him?" Maria asks.

"Not really. I just want to dance. I do like the way he danced Bachata. I like his style."

"Yeah, very sexy and smooth. Bachata is my favorite."

"Really? Salsa is my favorite. I can't dance it yet, but I love it." It's true. I love Salsa.

Bachata is fun, but the guy dances too close for me. It makes me feel claustrophobic. I have the gut reaction to push him away. I feel stifled like I can't fully express myself. Salsa is different. There is a balance of connection and freedom in which I am able to create more with my partner than I could alone. It's like he's giving me new ideas for the dance that I would have never found dancing by myself. I see the dance through his eyes and it awakens my own creativity. Empowered? I think that's the closest word I can find to explain it.

Now that the club is packed, I spend the rest of the night on the dance floor. Each guy represents another opportunity to learn. Luckily, as soon as I finish with one partner another quickly takes his place. I'm having fun, but over the course of the night, I start to notice an unsettling pattern. The guy dressed in white keeps reappearing. I'm so focused on dancing that I fail to realize that he keeps asking me to dance. It only becomes obvious when after dancing a song with him, I visit the Ladies Room, and when I come back out he is right there waiting for me. Cindy is right. He's giving me the creeps.

But since I try to follow the code of never turning down a dance, I follow him back onto the dance floor. It's another Bachata song. I'm guessing all of the songs we've danced together have been Bachata. I want to concentrate on the dance, but I'm distracted by an uncomfortable feeling. He stares at me, but doesn't smile. He feels too intense. There is an aggressiveness in the way he leans into me when we step backward or when he turns me into his arms. Finally, he says something in the middle of the song.

"Why can't you spin?"

I'm stunned. I feel like a fish that's been pulled out of the water. The air is sucked out. He's looking me dead in the eye.

"Your friends can spin. Even that girl over there can spin. They all can. It's easy. Why can't you?" His voice sounds gruff and agitated, as if I've wronged him somehow.

He starts dancing again when I say nothing. I don't know why, but I finish the dance. I feel too off balance emotionally to do anything else. At the end, I thank him like I do with everyone. Then I head off to the bathroom.

I stand there in front of the bathroom mirror trying to gather myself.

Cindy walks in.

"What's wrong?"

"I can't spin. The guy I was dancing with stopped me in the middle of the song to tell me I can't spin. He pointed out that you can spin. Maria can spin. And basically, everyone else in the club can spin, except me. And right now, I can't seem to get myself out of this bathroom."

Cindy looks pissed, but her voice remains calm, "Maybe I can give you some pointers. What happens when you spin?"

"I get dizzy."

"What you need to learn is how to spot. Have you ever watched ballerinas dance? They do this, so they don't get dizzy. You look at one spot, like your partner's face, and you keep your eyes on it even when your body starts the turn." As she tells me, she demonstrates it by moving her body in a slow turn. "You don't take your eyes off it until the last second and then you turn your head around fast, so your eyes can focus again on that one spot." Her body and head finish the turn at the same time. "Here, you try it."

"You're going to give me an emergency Salsa lesson in the Ladies Room?" I laugh.

"Yes, give me your hands. Step forward with your left foot. Look at me as you shift your weight to the right and start your turn. Don't look away, keep looking, keep looking." My body slowly turns to about the half way point. "Ok, turn your head quickly now. Look at me. Good!" My eyes land on her about the same time as my body completes the turn. My feet are a little wobbly on the finish, but I'm not dizzy.

"That really helps! Thank you. I think I'll need to practice it a lot. It doesn't feel natural, but I can see how it will help." Finally, I have something that might work.

"I also think you need to buy dance shoes. That will make a big difference in keeping your balance on the turns. Remember the shoes I showed you today? You can buy them online or there's a dance supply store in Santa Maria. You should pick up a pair."

"Okay, I can do that."

"And one more thing, let me watch you do your Salsa basic."

I perform the Salsa basic solo in the Ladies Room under Cindy's careful eye.

"I want you to point your toes outward," Cindy instructs. I follow her directions. "Let your feet make the letter "V" with your toes pointed out and your heels close together just like a ballerina. This will give you stability. See?" she gently pushes sideways on my right shoulder towards my midline, and I can still keep my balance. "Now put your feet back the way you danced before with the toes straightforward." She pushes again, and even though I know the push is coming, it throws me off easily. "Do you feel the difference?"

"I do. Thanks, I had no idea. I would've never thought of trying that."

"Every step you take I want your toes to keep pointing out. Especially when you step forward to make a spin, and when you complete the spin I want your toes to still point outwards to help with the finish."

I try to do my Salsa basic with my toes pointed outward. It feels awkward, but I have a feeling Cindy is right about it helping me with my balance.

"It feels harder to do my Salsa basic with my toes pointed out. I have to really concentrate or they start pointing straight ahead again, but I think your right about the balance. I'll have to practice."

"Yes, it feels unnatural at first. It will take time to get the hang of it, but the hard work will pay off. Are you ready to go back out there?" Cindy asks.

"Almost, I think I need a few more minutes to collect myself. Thanks for the emergency Salsa lesson," I can't help but laugh, and I give her a big hug.

After regaining my courage, I head back out. I see the guy in white waiting for me, but to my surprise Rick steps ahead of him and asks me to dance. His hand feels gentle and reassuring as he guides me back to dancing. I suspect this is Cindy's doing, and I'm grateful.

The night continues on. I try out Cindy's tips, but it's frustrating. Although it helps with the dizziness and balance, I feel like a newborn learning how to walk. I revert back to my old ways when I need to relax and enjoy the music, and then try the new technique when I get dizzy and off balance.

The guy in white reappears out of nowhere. Before he can ask me to dance, I approach another guy close by, and we head out onto the dance floor. I am done with the guy in white.

Cindy tells me around one in the morning that it's time to leave. I follow her over to our table to gather our things before heading out the door.

"You guys are leaving?" Maria asks.

"Yep, I have to work early tomorrow," Cindy replies and gives her a hug.

Maria gives me a big hug and her phone number.

As we leave the club, I turn to Cindy, "I didn't know you have to work early tomorrow. We didn't have to stay so late."

"You're not the only one addicted to dancing. Even after all these years, and all the clubs, I still love it."

I imagine I could be saying those exact words myself many years from now. We start the drive back to Cindy's place. The Salsa music playing in the background, as we laugh and share details of our best dances of the night.

Chapter 7 Dancing in Lompoc

"It's Thursday. Are you headed out to Santa Barbara for Salsa dancing after work?" Mike asks as he approaches the Front Desk.

"Nope. I'm not going this week."

"What? I'm surprised. I thought you were unstoppable," he gives me his handsome smile. How many of his female boot camp students wake up at six o'clock every Tuesday just to see that smile?

"I am unstoppable, but I'm going dancing on Saturday instead."

"Really? Where? Oxnard? LA?"

"No, Lompoc. We have a Salsa Night happening here. You should come. We need men."

"But I don't know how to dance," he glances down. I think this is the only time I've ever seen him not look confident.

"You can learn. There's a lesson at eight before the dancing starts. I've only seen one or two guys from Lompoc that know how to dance. Last time they had a couple of dancers from out of town visit. I don't know if they're coming back. If you learn how to dance, women will be desperate to dance with you."

"Really? So women like a guy who dances?" He teases.

"I haven't met one that doesn't. So will you come?"

"I was already planning on it, and I'm bringing a friend."

A friend? I wonder if his friend is a woman. Maybe a date?

"That's great." I try to sound casual. I'm not sure if I'm succeeding.

"This is a friend from back in my college days visiting for the weekend." He pauses before adding, "He's a Salsa dancer."

A Salsa dancer? Male? Jackpot.

"Really?"

"Yes, and he wants to meet you."

"You told him about me?" I'm not sure what to make of that.

"Of course, I told him I work with a beautiful woman who wants to learn how to dance Salsa."

"You didn't really say that."

"Something like that." Oh my goodness, with that smile of his I might have to start waking up at 6 a.m. for boot camp class.

"You know, I still can't dance. Last time I went was pretty horrific."

"Horrific?"

"Yeah, a guy stopped me mid-dance to ask me why I can't spin like everyone else. I felt really stupid."

"What did you say back to him?"

"Nothing."

"Why not?"

"I just couldn't."

"It would have been okay to tell him off."

"I know, and I don't know why I didn't."

"Don't let what he said get to you. I've seen you teach your classes. You're a natural dancer. It takes time to learn something new, but you will."

"Yeah, I know."

"If you see that guy again stay away from him. I know guys like that. They're no good."

"I will. But hey, let's get back to talking about Saturday. You're coming?"

"Yes."

"And you're going to take the lesson?"

"Yes, but don't expect much. Unlike you, I have two left feet and no rhythm."

"It doesn't matter all the women will be dying to dance with you."

"Really? All of them?" He raises an eye brow and shines his green eyes my way. I just laugh and leave it at that. He wanders off to lift weights.

The rest of the week flies by with the hustle and bustle of real life. I race from job to job, class to class, and spend time with my kids.

Saturday evening, I'm one of the first Lompocians to enter the Salsa Club. I don't want to be, especially since I'm walking in solo, but I am. I arrive early for every dance class. Even when I try to be late on purpose, I'm at least ten minutes early. It's an annoying habit I can't break.

Fortunately, I see Mike sitting at a table with his friend. I'd wager this is the sexiest table in the history of Lompoc. Mike is wearing a black dress shirt with black slacks that intensify his dark hair and green eyes. And of course, he is brandishing his trademark devilish smile. His friend is his equal in physical prowess wearing a white shirt and tan pants that accentuate his sandy blonde hair and brown eyes. And the fact that I already know he dances gives him an extra aura of sensuality. Both men are intoxicating to take in.

"Hello" I say as I make my approach.

"Here she is, the Amazing Scarlet," Mike announces as he stands up to offer me a seat.

"Scarlet, this is my friend, Pablo." Pablo rises to shake my hand.

"Nice to meet you, Scarlet," his voice is deep and soothing. I am the luckiest woman in Lompoc to be sitting with these guys.

"Nice to meet you too."

"Mike tells me you're learning how to dance Salsa?"

"I'm trying, but it's hard," I answer. It's also hard to look into Pablo's brown eyes without swooning. He reminds me of a young Robert Redford, the star of many classic films I watched as a teenager.

"It was hard for me too at first. Dancing Salsa takes a lot of practice. It's not as easy as it looks," Pablo shares as we sit down at the table.

"That's very true. How long have you been dancing?"

"Six years. If you take lessons, you'll learn faster. I took lessons for the first three years."

"I want to, but I don't know anyone who teaches in Lompoc. So, I take the lesson here once a month."

"That's a start," Mike chimes in.

As we talk, more people show up. I'm surprised. There's a good mix of men and women. I'd say most of the people here look to be in their thirties and forties. Everyone looks well-dressed and eager to start. Lompoc is Lompoc, and here everyone knows everyone, so there's comfortable chatter and hug exchanges as soon as someone new enters. Small town folk where no one is a stranger, at least not for long. If I don't know a person from elementary school or high school then I most likely know them from the gyms, or they know my mom, and if not from any of those associations then probably from a store I visit every week. It's smart to be nice to everyone in a small town, because there is no escaping them.

"If you're here for the Salsa lesson come out to the dance floor. We're about to start," a beautifully dressed woman makes the announcement. You can tell by her sparkly high heel shoes, tiny blue dress, and long curly red hair that she's the Salsa Instructor.

We gather together on the dance floor and form two lines. Somehow I find myself pushed into the front row, while Mike and Pablo find spots in the back.

"Are you guys ready to learn some Salsa?" The Salsa Instructor calls out as she takes the front.

There are a few whistles, cheers and claps. I try my best to yell out something and clap.

"My name is Suzy." A guy somewhere in the back row yells out, "Hi, Suzy."

"My job is to get you dancing. The first part of the class you'll be learning steps without a partner, and in the second half I'll teach you how to dance with a partner. Don't get frustrated if you have trouble catching on. It will take some practice, but tonight I will teach you the basics so we can get you moving," with that last bit she adds a little shoulder shimmy for fun. I like Suzy.

The footwork is easy for me. I catch on quickly. I know most of it from teaching the Latin aerobics classes, but I've also had a lot of practice in learning by following. My mother grew up in Hawaii. She started teaching me hula when I was about three years old. I have vivid memories of mimicking her steps as a child. I learned to memorize the moves quickly, because my mom kept changing the routine (which in hula you're not supposed to do). She tried to deny it, but later confessed she had trouble remembering the steps and told me to just follow. So, I did. Even when we would perform, I had to be ready for her improvisations. Now, that skill comes in handy whenever I learn something new.

Suzy is teaching us the Salsa basic, the forward together back together step we'll be using with our partners. We're learning how to do a right turn and a left turn. The right turn is the one that gets me dizzy when I dance with a guy, but doing it by myself seems a little easier. I'm trying to practice all of Cindy's tips for keeping my balance. Suzy also teaches us a step that matches her name called "Suzy Q." It's a twisty kind of double side step. She's put all of these moves into a little choreography so we can have something to practice. I glance behind me to spy on Pablo and Mike. It's obvious that Pablo knows what he is doing. He makes it look easy. Mike wasn't kidding. He really does have two left feet, and they seem to be working against each other.

"We're ready for music!" Suzy announces. She starts to tell the deejay to cue the music when three guys walk in. Esteban is standing there, and he's brought two friends.

"You made it," Suzy calls out to them.

"Yes, I'm sorry we're late. We hit some traffic," Esteban apologizes.

"Hey everyone. I'd like to introduce these guys to you. This is Esteban, Marco, and Fernando. They've come all the way from Oxnard to help me teach the class tonight. We're very lucky to have them." The guys are greeted by a round of clapping.

"We're just finishing up the first part of the lesson, and we'll have you guys join in for the second half with partnering," Suzy then turns back to us. "Okay, Deejay. We're ready!"

I feel a little nervous with Esteban watching. I wish I could move to the back row, but I'm stuck in the front. Suzy is upfront calling out the steps as she leads us. We're free to throw in our own shoulder shimmies and hip sways. I'm not sure if Esteban notices me because I don't dare look in his direction. I focus on what I always focus on when I dance with other people, the moment.

I've danced with a couple of performing hula groups, so I've danced in a lot of shows. I used to get stage fright, until one day I realized how lucky I was to be dancing with my friends. Who knows where life might take us next? So whenever I'm nervous, I remember that when the moment is gone it is gone forever. I'm trying to concentrate on that instead of Esteban standing there watching, the dancer I've been secretly searching for in every Salsa club.

When the song ends, we take a five-minute water break before the second part of the lesson begins. Esteban and his friends are talking to Suzy. Marco is the young one. He's in his early twenties and is dressed in a white t-shirt and jeans. Even though his dress is casual, he looks clean, trim, and well-mannered. Fernando appears to be more in his fifties, and is the only man in the room wearing a Fedora hat. Esteban is wearing a dark purple shirt and black slacks that accentuate his dark eyes and hair. I see other women staring at them too. I also notice Mike looking at me. Before I can read the expression on Mike's face, Suzy calls us back onto the dance floor.

We form two lines. The men are on one side, and the women line up facing them. Suzy has Esteban demonstrate the combinations with her and then the rest of us give it a try with our partner. She has us change partners frequently by calling out "Rotate" and signaling the women to move on to the next guy on the left.

I'd say there are at least a dozen dance partners in the line. This is a nice turn out. I'm in the middle of the room and to my left I see Marco and Esteban, and on my right, I find Pablo and Mike. The guy in front of me looks nervous. He's thinking so hard it's almost

45

painful to look at him. He's gripping my hands a little too much, but I don't think he realizes it. I offer a smile to help him relax.

"That's a lot to remember, huh?" I figure talking might help ease him.

"Yeah, this is my first time dancing," he replies.

"I haven't been dancing long either. I'm lucky that I just have to follow. I don't think I could remember all of those steps." Maybe voicing his fear out loud might make it less scary for him?

"I don't think I can either," he laughs a little and the tension in his face releases.

"That's ok. Whatever you remember will be more than I could." Finally, the death grip on my hands relaxes.

He does pretty good. We do a few Salsa basics, and a right hand turn which I manage without getting too dizzy. He then has me cross over to the other side and gives me another spin. He's delayed giving me the hand signals, and when he does he's a little rough pulling me along, but we muddle through and somehow end at the correct time. His face is sweating, but there is a look of utter relief. The teacher yells, "Rotate." I give him a high-five and move on to the next partner down the line which is Marco.

Marco doesn't say much, but I can feel in his hands that he is very relaxed. The teacher is having us do the same combinations, but with music this time. She warms us up with the Salsa basic so we can find the correct timing, and then she cues the steps. Marco is the smoothest dancer I've encountered. He is graceful, and when I dance with him I tap into that part of myself that learned to be graceful from dancing hula. When we finish the combinations, Marco keeps going. He's giving me a little extra to follow and enjoy. We stop only when the music stops. Then it's time for me to move on to the next guy.

Esteban takes both of my hands. The deejay starts the music again. We don't have time to talk before we're dancing together. I love the way his hands feel. I'm able to follow him better now after dancing with so many people. It's hard for me to look at him directly. He's the only dancer that makes me feel shy. Suzy calls out the steps and he leads me through them, but he adds little changes here and there. When we finish, he moves in close and kisses me on the cheek. I'm surprised by it. Kisses on the cheek are common in the Salsa world, but this felt different. This felt like something more.

"Rotate," Suzy calls out, and I have to move on. I dance with a few more guys, and Suzy keeps adding new steps to the routine. I eventually find my way to Pablo.

"Hi there, so how do you like Lompoc's Salsa Night?" I ask as he takes my hands.

"I'm having fun. I live in LA so this is a change of pace. The people here are friendly. It has a small town feel to it."

"I bet the dancers in LA are incredible." My mind conjures up visions of girls being flipped and twisted around in aerial spins.

"Yes, there are a lot of good dancers in LA, but I like this place. Everyone here is just starting to learn, so the people are nice and helping each other."

I am grateful for my little Lompoc. I complain that it's boring, and it seems as if I'm always trying to escape it in search of something else out there. But this is my home, and the people here are kind.

The music begins again. Pablo is plain fun. He leads the steps, but adds flourishes with shoulder shimmies and little guiding gestures that help me along in a friendly way. I find myself laughing as much as I am dancing. Too soon, our time together is over.

"Rotate! This is our final chance at this before the lesson is over," Suzy calls out. Finally, I'm partnered with Mike.

"How are your two left feet?" I tease.

"Confused," he laughs.

The music starts, and he takes my hands. We see each other almost every night at the gym, but we've never had any physical contact. For his first time dancing, he does a good job. I can tell he's memorized the steps even though I see him watching Esteban to find the right timing. His hands are a little rough, and when he motions me to walk across him he forgets to step out of the way so I can pass, but I just sidestep around him and find a path. When he goes to spin me he doesn't realize how tall he is and raises my arm really high which doesn't help with my balance issues, but at least I make it around and my eyes focus after a moment. When the music ends, I give him a hug. It's strange breaking through that professional barrier we keep at work, but here I let down my guard.

The lesson ends, and the real dancing starts. Esteban and Suzy take the floor. I can't help but watch. Whereas Marco is a graceful dancer and Pablo is pure fun, Esteban has charisma. Your eye is drawn to him. The dance floor could be crowded with dancers, but he's the one that captures the attention. I think it's his creativity. He has an unending supply of combinations. Esteban just explodes with a variety of moves. It looks like he could go on forever.

My watching is interrupted by Pablo.

"Would you like to dance?" He asks.

It's intimidating entering the dance floor with Esteban and Suzy, but Pablo puts me at ease by flashing a goofy expression. It tells me whatever this is, it will be fun. He spins me around and catches me before I can feel off balance. There is no time to think, because he already has me moving. Whenever I start to get nervous, he makes a silly face. My body is loose and free to ad lib with moves from my Latin dance classes. Pablo lets me be myself. He has me twirling and traveling all over the place. Before I can get disoriented he appears out of nowhere to focus me. I can do no wrong. He throws my arm in the air and then spins and catches me and takes me into a dip, but before I can panic about being in a dip he brings me up to him so fast that my long hair flies up adding drama. He creates the illusion that I know how to dance. The crowd is not only watching Esteban and Suzy, but us as well.

He lets go of my hands so we can dance solo. This is my strength. I'm no longer constrained by someone else's interpretation of the music. I also feel challenged. Even though the odds are against me, I want my partner and I to either hold our own or out dance Esteban and Suzy. Pablo doesn't have Esteban's charisma, but his sense of humor shines in his steps. His moves are flawless, but done in a manner that he could care less if they weren't. There's a playfulness that is infectious. The bystanders love it.

He calls me back to him by offering his hand. I throw myself into a spin to face him and lightly place my hand into his to accept the invitation. He nods and smiles at the unexpected flair. We finish the song together. I give him a high five.

I walk over to Mike, and Pablo finds another girl.

"You were beautiful out there," Mike tells me, but then having said the words his eyes dart away.

"Would you like to dance?" I ask.

"No," he shakes his head, "I'm not ready." I'm disappointed, but I understand.

"That's okay. When you're ready, we'll dance. It's a lot to learn, huh? I still get dizzy," I'm going to say more, but I'm cut off.

"Mike, dance with me!" One of his boot camp students runs up to him and grabs both of his hands. I don't recognize her at first in her dress, heels, and blonde hair hanging in loose curls past her shoulders. I'm used to seeing her at six in the morning with no makeup, a ponytail, and clothes covered with sweat. She is in her early twenties and very pretty. Mike keeps saying no as she pulls him out to the dance floor. She is not letting him go.

The night continues on. I dance with a few guys, but mostly with Pablo. He is doing me a favor by giving me pointers on how to read the guy's hand signals. I'm grateful for the instruction. Poor Mike keeps getting dragged out to the dance floor by woman after woman. They could care less if he has two left feet. This is their one shot at being close to the Greek God who roams the gym, and they are not missing it. I feel bad for him, but I can't stop laughing each time I see it happen. Esteban dances with all the girls. I love watching him, but he has yet to ask me for a dance.

After only an hour, Pablo tells me they are leaving. My guess is that Mike can't endure it any longer.

"Thanks, Pablo, for everything. I learned a lot from you tonight," I tell him.

He pulls me in for one last hug, "Call me when you're ready to dance in LA."

"I will," I promise. I turn to Mike, "You survived!"

"Barely," he shrugs his shoulders.

"I was a little scared for you," I tease.

"Me too."

"You made a lot of women happy tonight," I tell him. He looks miserable. We exchange a hug, and say goodnight.

Mike and Pablo leave, but the night is just beginning. As soon as they're gone, I see Esteban from across the room start to move towards me. Am I imagining it? Is there another girl close to me? I try to look around without being obvious, but no. It's just me.

"Do you want to dance?" He offers his hand. I accept.

Chapter 8 Dance with Me

This is what I've been searching for in every dance. Esteban pushes me past what I think I am capable of doing. He doesn't spin me once, but twice. The timing is different too. Its accelerated. We're on beat, but the spins are slightly faster so we can have a distinct pause on the fourth and eighth beats. Most guys hold back with me because they can see I'm a beginner, which honestly, is what good dancers are taught to do. The leader dances at the level of the follower. Esteban breaks this rule. He dances beyond me, and I love it.

I know there is no way I can do everything he's signaling me to do, but I go for it. There's that thought of "What if?" What if I make this double spin? What if I can move this fast? What would it be like if I could keep up with him? Be better than him? What would it feel like? That is the challenge, and I love to be challenged. I'm being pushed to the edge of what I can do, and I'm not sure what will happen. The ghost of myself that haunts me says, "Why not try?"

Esteban's face lights up when he dances. There is a mischievous look in his eye when he's about to do something crazy like letting me go into a fast spin only to drop down to the ground and pop up to surprise me when I stop. Everything feels spontaneous. I suspect he's making it up as we go along. By the end of the song, I have to catch my breath. He follows me off the dance floor.

"Did your boyfriend have to leave early?" He asks.

"Boyfriend?" I'm confused, but then remember dancing with Pablo earlier. "I don't have a boyfriend," I answer.

"I'm sorry. I thought the guy you were dancing with was your boyfriend."

"No, I just met him tonight. He was helping me learn."

51

"Do you want to learn how to dance?"

"Yes, I love Salsa," I say as we move further away from the dance floor.

"I could teach you," he offers.

"Really?" I'm excited. After spending time in the Salsa clubs, I am convinced this is the guy who can bring out the best in me. He has a speed and creativity that I don't see in the other dancers. I know I have it in me too, untapped and waiting. Plus, I feel drawn to him.

"Yes, I can teach you. The two guys here with me tonight, Marco and Fernando, are my students. They've only been dancing for a couple of months. I also teach some other people back in Oxnard."

I'm impressed. Marco already dances better than most of the guys I've found in the clubs. I can't believe he has learned that much in a couple of months.

"I'd love that," I answer.

"Can I get you a drink?" He offers as he leads me towards the bar.

"Water would be great."

"Just water?"

"Yes, it's the only thing I drink when I go dancing. I never drink alcohol. I'm not against it, and I don't have a drinking problem. I just don't like how it slows me down."

He orders water for me and a soda for himself. We find a table in the back of the restaurant away from the dance area.

Esteban asks me a lot of questions. If I have kids, what I do for a living. I tell him about the divorce, my two boys, and all of my jobs. He shares with me about himself too. That he's never been married, has no children and has worked at the same retail store for fifteen years. In a short amount of time, he has covered most of the basic information.

Esteban is my only exception to the three dance rule. We dance together the rest of the night. He starts holding my hand even when the songs are over. Lucky for me I exercise for a living, otherwise my body couldn't withstand the nonstop cardio of dancing with him for hours. At some point though, we do go outside and walk around the club to talk and get fresh air.

We hold hands as we walk along the outside of the building.

"How long have you been dancing?" I ask.

"I danced for four years and then stopped. I came back to it about a year ago. I had a hard time learning," he laughs.

"You did?"

"Yes, no one had a harder time learning to dance than me. Do you know how long I went to the clubs before I asked the first girl to dance?" He asks as he looks at me.

"How long?"

"Guess."

"A month?"

"Longer."

"Three months?"

"No, six months. I went to the clubs for six months before I asked the first girl to dance," he tells me.

I visualize myself entering the Havana Night Club and being carried off to the dance floor by the deejay as soon as I walked in. I've been dancing nonstop ever since.

"The first girl I asked to dance was mean. She told me I didn't know how to dance at all."

"That's awful," I say as I remember the guy in white from La Pura Vida.

"So I started taking lessons, but I didn't learn anything. I spent a lot of money, but nobody could teach me. I was that bad." He's saying this to me, but I have a hard time accepting it.

"But, I eventually found someone who could teach me."

"Who?"

"Luis Chavez, he's a ten-time World Champion. Luis was able to teach me to dance," Esteban smiles and moves closer to me. "I took lessons for a few years, but then I stopped."

"Why?" I ask.

"I wanted to make more money. I was traveling to LA four times a week for lessons and working three jobs. Often I wouldn't make it home from the clubs until four in the morning. I was exhausted. I took a break so I could focus on getting ahead financially, but about a year ago I returned to dancing. I only work one job now so I have more time."

We walk around the shopping center that shares the parking lot with La Casa Roja. In front of the old movie theater, Esteban leans against the wall, and pulls me towards him. He places his hands softly around my face.

"You're beautiful. You do know that," he looks into my eyes.

"No," I look downwards and shake my head. The word comes out before I can correct it. I've always liked the way I look and wouldn't want to change anything, but I don't feel beautiful. I feel damaged.

I pull away. He gently takes my hand again, and we walk around the closed shops.

"Do you go dancing anywhere?" He asks.

"Yes, I've started going to the Havana Night Club in Santa Barbara on Thursdays."

"Are you going this Thursday?"

"Yes."

"I'll meet you there," he smiles at me.

"I'd like that," I can feel myself smiling back at him. I have a date with Esteban.

Chapter 9 Meet Me in Havana

"You look happy," Angie tells me as she walks up to me at Women4Fitness. She is my favorite gym member. Angie and I have similar body types and are almost the same height. She's maybe a little taller. She has short blonde hair and pretty blue eyes that light up when she laughs, which is often. Angie makes me laugh more than anyone I've ever met. Angie has a big heart, and she is quick to find humor in even the most trying situations. Given my life after the divorce, I treasure her friendship.

"I think someone has met a guy," she probes a little.

"Yes, and I have a date with him tonight. And you won't believe this," I pause for drama, "he can dance." I feel like a teenager telling my best friend that I'm going on my first date.

"Oh, that's wonderful! I'm so happy for you! How did you two meet?"

"Last Saturday, at the Salsa Night here in Lompoc," as I say the words I see her surprise.

"Here in Lompoc?" She asks.

"Yes, he came from Oxnard to help with the Salsa Night. Believe me, if a guy walks into Lompoc and can dance like him, he's mine! When will I ever see another one?" We both laugh. We tell the dumbest jokes and find them funny.

"So where is he taking you?"

"We're meeting at the Havana Night Club in Santa Barbara. I'm so excited!" It's nice to share my excitement with someone. I've been keeping it to myself all week.

"What are you going to wear?" She asks.

"I think I'll wear my red dress," I answer. I love talking to Angie, because she brings out the kid in me. Normally, I couldn't care less what I wear since I'm always working out, but with Angie it's fun talking about frivolous stuff like what to wear on a date.

"Red is the perfect color for you," she wants to say more but my Get Fit appointment has arrived. Not wanting to delay me with my client she heads off with "I want details tomorrow!"

The more excited I get about my date, the slower the day drags. Still, since time can't stop completely I eventually make it through the rest of my Get Fit appointments. I'm down to my last fifteen minutes of work at the Lompoc Valley Gym.

"Hey there!" Mike says as I find him practically nose to nose with me. I've been daydreaming. I'm resting my chin on my hands with my elbows on the counter. He's mimicking my pose, elbows and all.

"Hi," I manage to squeak out even though I'm startled.

"You look lost in space. Are you thinking about dancing?" He asks.

He knows me. I'm predictable.

"Yes," I answer.

"It's Thursday night, huh?" He says these words a little slow and drawn out.

"Yes, it is."

"Are you going dancing in Santa Barbara?"

"Of course!" I reply as I finally lift my head off my chin. I can't take him being nose to nose with me anymore. He wins.

"Do you ever get nervous making the drive by yourself late at night?" Mike's tone turns from playful to more serious.

"A little, but I don't let it stop me."

"If you want, I could come with you. I can't dance, but I can be your driver."

57

It's a generous offer, but even if I wasn't meeting Esteban tonight I would turn it down. It doesn't feel right.

"No, it's okay. I have a friend that meets me at the club, so I'm not there by myself. Thanks for offering though, it means a lot." I purposely leave out whether my friend is male or female.

"All right, but the offer still stands if you change your mind." He waits a second and adds, "Be careful out there." Mike gives me one of his smiles, but there is an undertone of concern in his eyes.

I am careful, and I make it to the Havana Night Club safely. I check myself in the rear view mirror making sure my makeup is perfect. I don't know what to expect. I don't know if Esteban is already inside waiting for me. My nerves are bubbled up. After twenty years of marriage, dating is foreign territory. But like every night time venture, the ghost of myself whispers, "What the hell are you waiting for? Go inside already!"

I don't have to walk far into the club before Esteban finds me. He embraces me with a hug and a kiss on the cheek.

"Come with me. I have something for you," he takes my hand and leads me back outside. We walk out to his car.

"When did you get to the club? You haven't been waiting long, have you" I ask.

"I arrived ten minutes ago, so not too long," he answers as he reaches into the back seat of his car. He brings out a bouquet of a dozen roses.

"They're beautiful! Thank you," I kiss his cheek. I don't care how old I am this old fashion gesture makes me feel special. Something I haven't felt for a long time. We put the flowers in my car and return to the club.

He takes me onto the dance floor, and we get lost in it all. The music, the lights, and the people dancing around us are like an ocean of pure energy. He has my full attention as I try to follow him. He moves faster than the rest of the men on the dance floor. I'm dancing on the tightrope of being able to handle it or falling down. The risk of falling is a real possibility. I could ask him to slow down, but doing so would ruin it for me. I'm learning at warp speed, and I love it. Out of the corner of my eye, I start to notice the bright light of a cell phone recording us. It's the promoter. He's walking around the club. I see his light shine on us for quite some time before moving on.

I'm not sure how many songs we dance before we take a break, but eventually we head outside to the courtyard and stand by the fire.

"Finally! I can say hello to you! You've been dancing nonstop," Cindy comes up and gives me a hug.

"I'm sorry. I started dancing and lost track of everything," I apologize.

"No worries. It happens to me all the time!" Cindy laughs. She turns to Esteban, "I see you out dancing everywhere, hello" Cindy gives him a hug too.

"Hello, how are you?" Esteban asks.

"I'm good," Cindy gives me a look that says "I'm going to ask you a million questions", but before she can utter a single word a guy asks her to dance.

"People are not used to seeing me with a date in the clubs," Esteban tells me.

"Really?" I ask. I imagine there are many girls who have wanted to have a date with him dancing.

"Yeah, I never date the girls from Salsa. I go dancing all the time, but I'm never with anyone. So, this is new to me."

"Cindy doesn't seem to date guys from Salsa either. Why is that?"

"That's because everyone talks in Salsa."

"How so?" I ask.

"If you're dating someone and break up, everyone talks about it. If you're dating someone, and you go out dancing alone people will make up stories even if you've done nothing wrong. For instance, if we're dating you could go out with some friends dancing, and in Salsa everyone dances with everyone, and I guarantee you I would have people try to cause trouble between us by telling me lies or exaggerating things."

"They really do that?" I'm skeptical of what he is saying. I'm not used to someone causing trouble for no reason.

"Yes," Esteban answers.

I'm surprised by our conversation. I wasn't expecting this. I start to walk around the patio. He follows.

"Do you come to this club often?" I ask.

"No, this is my first time. I usually dance in Oxnard or LA. I do come to Santa Barbara once in a while, but never here." He takes my hand in his as we stroll around the courtyard.

We enter the club from the other side entrance. It has a separate dance floor, and the music here is different. It's Cumbia.

Cumbia music has its own sweet flavor. Whereas Salsa challenges me and Bachata is sexy, Cumbia has a heartfelt quality that reminds me of everything good in life. In Salsa, partners move forward and back for their basic step. The Bachata basic has the couples dancing from side to side. Both dances are mostly linear in the footwork. Cumbia has some linear movements, but also adds circular patterns as the couple rotates around each other spinning. It feels like a carnival ride as you whizz around your partner. The leader grips the hand a little stronger than in the other dances. My guess is so you won't go flying off the ride when you hit top speed. I've only tried it a couple of times. I find it easier to dance than Salsa.

This dance area is crowded. The two dance floors are on opposite ends, and there's no wall separating them just a long bar that extends the length of the club. I don't recognize any of the dancers. I guess those who love Salsa and Bachata stay primarily on one side, and those who love Cumbia dance here.

Esteban leads me onto the Cumbia floor, and we join in. Esteban is more relaxed dancing Cumbia. On the Salsa floor, there is an undercurrent of competition among the good male dancers, each trying to out dance the others. There is pressure for the women to read the hand signals correctly, especially when the combinations get complicated. Not so here. The music almost invites you to drink a beer before heading out to dance, and I suspect most of the men around me have been hanging out at the bar all night. I even see some guys singing to the women as they dance together. Esteban is still a fast dancer, but his moves are more repetitive in Cumbia, and I can follow them easily. It's fun twirling around him. He has a little jump in some of his moves, and I experiment with adding some of my own jumps along with him. We lose track of time as one song blends into another, but at some point the music comes to an end, and he brings me close for a kiss. I'm caught off guard and the moment is gone before I can realize what has happened.

He leads me outside again to sit under the stars. The cool air feels sweet on my skin after the dancing. The club is approaching the closing hour.

"Are you free this Saturday?" He asks.

"Not this Saturday, but the following weekend my boys are with their father. I'd be able to do something then."

"That would work. I thought I might visit you in Lompoc."

"I'd love that. What do you want to do?" I ask.

"Whatever you want. I'll head up in the morning, and we can spend the day together. I'll have to leave before five, because my family is having a fiesta that evening to celebrate a birthday."

"That would be fun," I try not to sound as excited as I feel.

"I haven't seen Lompoc except for the Salsa Night."

"Well, it's a small town."

"That's what I like about it."

"Okay, maybe we'll go to La Purisma Mission. It's one of my favorite places," as I finish the words he kisses me. The world pauses. I give into my senses. The touch of his lips, the smell of his cologne, the background Salsa music, the light breeze of the night air, and the exploration of someone new. I give myself fully to taking it in, to knowing him. I can feel the questions he wants to ask, and give my answers without saying a word. When our lips part again, there remains a connection that didn't exist before.

On my long drive home, I replay that kiss a dozen times. The ghost of myself that shares the car ride home leans back in her seat, puts her feet up on the dashboard and tells me, "This is only the beginning."

Chapter 10 La Purisma Mission

He calls me every night. I love ending my day talking to him. It's perfect. I work, exercise, spend time with my boys, clean as much as I can, and when I head to bed the phone rings around ten. I have someone to share my day with before I fall asleep. I'm trying not to look forward to it too much, because who knows how long it will last, but I do secretly hope every night that he will call.

I checked Facebook the day after the Havana Club. The club promoters post pictures and videos on their Facebook page. They might catch you in mid spin with your eyes closed, or they could get a great shot of you that makes you look like a real dancer. I've had both. What I found this time was special.

It was a video of Esteban and I dancing together. We stand out amongst the multi-colored strobe lights with his white shirt and my red dress. The way I look on the dance floor is very different than what I experience as a dancer. While I dance I'm struggling to read the hand signals, find the timing, and battle the dizziness from spinning, but on the video I look beautiful. It is the ghost of myself caught on camera, and she is graceful and mesmerizing. She makes it look easy, like she was made to dance. Esteban is quick on his feet, and he keeps me moving and twirling about him. The video is only thirty seconds long, but I can't count how much time I've spent re-watching it.

My kids have already left for their father's for the weekend. I miss them terribly, but I need this alone time. I've tried my best to keep it together around them. I remember my parents' divorce being a battlefield. I want to spare my kids that nightmare. I can't control what their father chooses to bring into their lives, but I can create a safe haven they can come home to and find peace. To do that, I have to take care of myself. I know I'm a mess on the inside, no matter what I might look like on the outside.

Esteban should be here any minute. I'm waiting for him at the Home Depot parking lot. It's a good place to meet, because it's easily visible as you enter the town. I'm nervous. I've tried on five different outfits, and I'm still not sure I picked the right one. His white car pulls up in front of mine. Here goes nothing. I hop out of my car and into his.

"Hello," he greets me with a sweet kiss.

"How was the drive?" I ask.

"Nice, I saw a lot of cows." We laugh. It's true. I guess it would be a surprise after living in Oxnard and driving along the 101 Highway. You're not expecting the cows.

He wants a tour of the town, so we take the long route to the Mission. Our town has only two main streets "H" and "Ocean". I figure we'll make it to the Mission within fifteen minutes, and that's only because it's on the outskirts of town and we're taking the scenic route. Whenever a visitor asks me for directions and then wants to know how long it will take to get to their destination, my answer is always the same, five minutes. I don't care if it's on the other side of town, five minutes.

I point out our town murals. Little Lompoc has artists create huge wall murals that you'll find on random buildings depicting the history of the area. It's a quirk that I love. We have thirty-six murals decorating the town.

Most of the buildings look like they've come from the 1960s. Lompoc hasn't changed much since my childhood days, except we do have more shops. From talking to the old timers and the young ones, I figure all children growing up in Lompoc have a similar experience regardless of the generation. We cruise "H" and "Ocean" when we're teenagers, look forward to the Flower Festival in June to see our school friends, and live in a town where everyone knows either us or our parents.

64

We pass by La Casa Roja and the old drive in movie theater that is now a recycling center. Then we make a right onto a country road that leads to the Mission. As we drive, I point out a road to our left that leads to my parents' land in the country. They have a twenty-acre lot in Cebada Canyon. My stepfather loves to grow grapes and make wine. He's been growing his own grapes since the 1970s. His wine hobby is now in vogue. Who knew Lompoc would become part of the California winery heartland?

"Just turn in here," I tell Esteban when I see the entrance to the Mission. We find a parking space and get ready to explore. It's another perfect California day. The sun is shining and the skies are blue. Walking into the Mission is like walking into the past, or at least, a re-creation of the past. La Purisma Mission is one of twenty-one Spanish Missions built in California between the years 1769 and 1833.

Esteban takes my hand. We cross over the little wooden bridge and into a vast open field. In the distance, we see a large pink building with three arches that houses three bells and is topped with a cross. It is attached to the Mission cemetery on one side, and a long white building on the other. As a child, the sight of the cemetery both excited and frightened me. As an adult, it reminds me that life is too short. To the right of us, there is a large fenced area where the animals roam. The big black bull with his long horns can be seen close by.

"This is my favorite guy," I tell Esteban as we near the fence.

"He's big. What a beautiful animal!"

"I can't remember a time when I didn't see him here. I think everyone in Lompoc knows him."

We continue to make our way around the fence admiring the sheep and donkeys.

"I've been coming to this Mission since I was seven. I think most of the kids who grow up in Lompoc have memories of this place. The first time I came here I saw a snake."

"There are snakes here?" He asks.

"Yep, so you do have to watch your step. Most of the time, you don't see any, but my first time here I saw one up there," I point to a little hill with a large wooden cross sitting on its peak.

"You can't go up there now, but when I was a kid you could walk up to the top of that hill and that's where I saw the big snake. I was with my mother and we ran down the hill screaming," I can't help but laugh remembering it.

We make our way over to the pink building with its cemetery. It's basically an open structure with no ceiling. The four walls enclose the Mission burial ground. It's always given me an eerie feeling knowing that there were others here before me, seeing the same sun and blue skies, and that they are still here in one way or another. Esteban and I walk through the buildings of the Mission stopping to read the signs that describe each room.

"I hope this isn't boring for you," I wonder if this small town stuff is too slow for him. I imagine there must be more exciting things to do or see in Oxnard.

"No, I like it. I'm always working or dancing at the clubs. I never get a chance to be outside and see anything new. It's also nice to be away from crowds of people," Esteban tells me as we continue sightseeing.

"You know this is not the original mission. The first mission was destroyed by an earthquake in 1812, and they rebuilt a new mission here. I'll show you the original site some time. It's in town not far from my house. There's not much left of it, just a couple of walls. I saw it for the first time a couple of weeks ago. I had recalled hearing about it as a kid so I asked around to find out where it was, and I had to search a bit to find it, but there it was close to home."

He takes my arm as we walk and links it in his. He also switches sides with me, placing me closer to the buildings. It feels very old fashion.

"In my family, I was taught to walk with a girl this way," Esteban shares with me. "The guy walks on the outside by the street so he can protect his date from any danger." I don't know what to say. I let my body slide closer to him. I turn my head slightly away to hide my smile.

We open the large wooden doors to enter the main church. The light comes in behind us to illuminate the wide space and shines upon the portrait I've been waiting to show him.

"This is my favorite painting," I point to the large picture across the room which shows a man dressed in black robes surrounded by baby cherubs. There is a distressed look on the man's face that puzzles me. What has he done to be in such a predicament? Surrounded by baby cherubs but looking tormented. The portrait is done in dark colors which deepen the despair. If art is meant to make you feel something when you look at it, then this has been art to me since I was a child.

"This painting has always fascinated me, and scared me a little. Every time I visit the Mission it is the one thing I have to see."

"It's powerful," Esteban says as he looks up at the painting. "I can't tell if he's begging the cherubs for help or if he's terrified of them."

"You're right. The look on his face could mean so many things. Is he scared, angry, or desperate?"

"Maybe all of the above?" Esteban puts his arms around me. I nestle in close to him.

"I've never thought of that. You might be on to something," as I finish my words, Esteban stays quiet.

I can see him taking in the place from the altar with its statues to the signs of the cross adorning the walls to the confessional where once long ago people lined up to share their sins.

"I haven't been in a church for many years," Esteban tells me.

"Are you Catholic?" I ask.

"Yes, but I've worked weekends for the past fifteen years so I haven't gone to Mass. This place brings back memories of going to church with my Grandma when I would visit her in Mexico as a little boy." We linger in the church for a while taking in the architecture, childhood memories, and thoughts of others before us that worshipped here over two hundred years ago.

We venture back outside and I take him over to see the pigs and roosters, and then we visit the garden. It has a display of all the vegetation that was common in the 1800s. I don't know much about plants, but I can still appreciate their beauty on a sunny day.

I lead us over to the large water fountain that stands in the middle of the garden. It's gently covered in shade from the nearby trees. I dig through my purse and hand Esteban a penny.

"You have to make a wish," I tell him.

"A wish?" He raises his eyebrows and gives me a smile.

"It's a tradition. I never pass this without making a wish. My boys and I usually make about four or five wishes each when we visit."

He places one hand on the side of my face, and then leans in to kiss me slowly. How many pennies have been tossed into the water wishing for this?

"Are you hungry?" He asks.

"Yes," I answer as I collect myself.

"Where can I take you for lunch?"

"Have you ever been to Solvang?" I ask.

"No," Esteban answers and I can tell by the surprised look on his face that he hasn't even heard of the Danish town.

"It's about twenty minutes from here, and I think you'll like it especially if you never get to see anything new. Do you want to go there for lunch?"

"Yeah, that sounds good."

"Let's go then," I take his hand and we leave the Mission behind. We head off to another hometown treasure.

We drive up Highway 246, passing the wineries lining up the sides of the road with their tidy rows of grapevines. We pass the little town of Buellton with its classic green and white Pea Anderson Soup billboard and find our way to Solvang.

This little town was built in 1911 by a group of Danish settlers. The architecture shows their Danish handprint. I love visiting because it feels like walking into a fairytale in the middle of California. Throughout the years, I've collected trinkets from the shops such as my yearly Christmas ornament, gnomes, music boxes, and even my wedding veil.

I have Esteban park far away from the restaurant, so we can meander down the main street before stopping for lunch. We step out of the car and into a Danish village. The shops line the streets selling a variety of wares, everything from Danish souvenirs to New Age crystals. Each shop is unique, but all are housed in a Danish style building that blends with the rest. The town is complete with windmills and Clydesdale horses that give carriage rides up and down the streets.

We find our way to the Danish restaurant for lunch. Its décor hasn't changed much since I was a kid, and I think that's because none of us would ever want it to. It has wooden booths with orange vinyl padding that are lined up against the walls. There are touches of Denmark to be seen from the photos to the menu which is written in both Danish and English.

Esteban has me enter the booth first and then he slides in next to me. He stretches a little and lifts his sweater which shows his six pack. It's done in a subtle way as if he's not really showing it to me directly, but I'm guessing I'm meant to see it. I'm surprised. This is out of character for him. I can't resist the effect it has on me.

"What do you think of Solvang?" I ask.

"I like it. I've never been this far North. I'm usually working, and when I do go somewhere it's LA."

"I've lived in a few places. When I was married my husband's job required us to move a lot. I became addicted to the nomadic lifestyle. No matter how happy I was in one place, I always had the itch to move somewhere new. When I came home to California and saw the Pacific Ocean along Highway 101, I finally felt settled. This is where I want to stay."

"Do you know what I want?" Esteban says as he turns towards me. "I want to have my own dance company, and then one day create a dance academy where anyone can learn to dance."

"What kinds of dance would you teach?"

"I would teach Salsa, but I wouldn't be the only teacher. I would hire other instructors. I want to have everything there from ballet to ballroom."

"I like that. It sounds exciting. So, you're teaching in Oxnard?"

"Yes, I used to teach at a dance studio in Ventura. The class was really big, but my work schedule kept changing so I couldn't keep it going. I hated giving it up. But six months later, a friend asked me to teach him and a couple of his friends at his house. He has an area outside in his backyard set up that we use. Right now, we have four guys and three girls. We practice four days a week. Marco teaches the class when I can't make it."

"Marco is a good dancer. I can't believe he's only been dancing for a few months. Did he dance something else before?"

"Nope. It's all in the practice. Most people take too many lessons learning fancy combinations when they should spend their time practicing the basics. You learn much faster."

"I wish I could go to your practices in Oxnard."

"You can practice on your own. Next time I visit I can teach you what to practice."

"Would you? I really want to learn," as I say this I think about how having a dance lesson with Esteban would be the best date ever.

"Sure. Besides learning how to dance, do you have anything else your working towards?"

"Yes, I want to be a Personal Trainer. I'm studying to take the exam to be certified. I love helping people work towards their goals. For me, the fun part is when I see the transformation. They don't just lose weight or gain muscle. It's like they come alive again and it affects more than just a physical change. They start trying new things from how they dress to taking up a hobby they've always wanted to try," as I share this my mind shows me several women I've seen take such a journey. The hobbies they pick up are always a surprise, anything from photography to cello lessons. Regular exercise gives them the extra energy needed at the end of the day to have a life. The commitment to improving their health reinforces the idea that they matter, and have a right to do something that makes them happy.

"Like how you've taken up Salsa dancing?"

"I guess so," now that he points it out I see the obvious connection. What I want most for others, I desperately need for myself.

"Why do you want to learn to dance Salsa?" Esteban asks.

"I'm not sure. I'm just drawn to it,' I give him a half answer. I can't fully explain the attraction. Something about the music makes sense to me, although I don't understand many of the words. The music invites my body to move the way it's always wanted to, even if it has no idea how to just yet. And then there is dancing with a partner, the connection. Tapping into someone else's ideas of what the dance should be and then reacting to it spontaneously. I guess it's the combination of impermanence and permanence. The spontaneity of the dance that embodies only a brief space in time juxtaposed upon bringing something of out of myself that has always been there lying below the surface waiting to be seen.

We spend the rest of the day in Solvang. Cruising along the streets and sightseeing in the shops. Esteban walking on the outside by the street with his arm linked in mine.

This day together is like a dance, a moment in time shared which I appreciate because I realize it will not last. Divorce teaches you that. Whoever you are with enjoy your time with them. A relationship lives in the here and now, and is not protected by labels such as boyfriend/girlfriend or husband/wife. Its life span is fragile. Even if it lasts twenty, fifty, or seventy years, it will be gone too soon. So, I let myself have this. I forget my troubles, and feel so lucky to spend the day with Esteban.

Chapter 11 So You Want to Dance?

"Tell me all about it," Cindy begins the interrogation. It's just her and I sitting under the greenery at the Havana Night Club in an outside booth with its soft candlelight setting. I've been dancing with men all night, and now that it's approaching the closing hour Cindy has cornered me for answers.

I share with Cindy how Esteban and I met. I even give her highlights of our day together in Lompoc.

"Why didn't he meet you here tonight?" She asks.

"His group practices on Thursday nights, but he's coming up this Saturday to teach me how to dance. I'm trying to get in all the practice that I can."

"He's a good dancer, but he does have a couple of problems with his dancing," Cindy tries to break this to me gently. I can see by the way she is choosing her words carefully that she's trying to be honest and not hurt my feelings at the same time.

"What problems does he have?" I keep my voice calm and fight down the urge to be defensive. I know Cindy's advice comes with good intentions.

"Esteban doesn't dance on beat. He strays from it when he does a lot of combinations. He's also hard to follow. I've seen very few who could follow him when he dances fast. I have a rough time following him," as Cindy shares her concerns she watches for my reaction.

"Okay, maybe that's true, but I still think I can learn a lot from him. Marco has only been taking lessons from him for three months, and he's amazing." I refrain from telling Cindy what I really think. I'm not a Salsa expert, but I trust my instincts when it comes to dancing. I don't think Esteban has trouble keeping the beat. I think he just hasn't met a girl yet who can react fast enough to his

73

signals. The delayed reaction slows him down and ruins whatever he had planned.

"It's not just about the dancing," Cindy takes a small breath before continuing on. "Most relationships don't last in Salsa."

"Why is that?" I ask.

"Who knows really, but this is what I think. These guys are used to dancing with a variety of beautiful women. Some of these Salseros go out dancing three to four times a week. I know guys in the club right now who have been dancing for five, ten or fifteen years. That lifestyle would be a lot to give up for one woman. Either she would have to be a dancer herself and be very resistant to jealousy or the Salsero would have to be willing to change. You can probably already feel how addictive dancing can be, the excitement is like a drug. I see girls date the good dancers and they seem to be happy at first. But after a while, the lifestyle wears them down. It's hard to see the man of your dreams dancing with other beautiful women night after night." Cindy is a straight shooter. She's telling me exactly like it is even though I can see she doesn't want to hurt me.

"Do the men tend to cheat? Or is it really just about the dancing for them? When I dance with men I'm all about the dancing. I barely notice what they look like. So far, Esteban is the only one I've been attracted to so cheating wouldn't be an issue for me. What about the guys? Are they the same way?" I give voice to the question running around in my head.

"I'm sure some are exactly like you. It's all about the dancing for them. But the truth is that a lot of the guys do cheat, I've seen it happen many times. I'd say in most cases, the couple just breaks up for one reason or another, and then the guy moves on to another girl. I see this with many of the instructors. If a guy can dance, he will always have women who want to be with him. Salsa is a small world. If you two break up, you'll have to deal with seeing Esteban with other women or give up dancing."

"Is that why you never date anyone from Salsa?"

"Yes, I've seen this scenario repeated so many times I don't like the odds. I'd rather keep dancing fun and drama free. As for dating non-dancers, that's tough too. Most boyfriends have a hard time understanding my need to dance. At first, they might seem okay with it, especially since having a girlfriend who can dance is very sexy, but eventually they just want someone to be home with them at night. You know, like have a normal life with a partner to watch TV, say goodnight to in bed, and make love when the mood strikes. Not a woman that comes home at two in the morning after dancing with man after man while her boyfriend has spent the night alone waiting for her."

"You can't give dancing up. Can you?" I feel worried for my friend. Is she happy?

"No, I wouldn't recognize myself if I did." Cindy says this without emotion. It's something she must have realized about herself and accepted.

Have I gone too far already? Could I give it up? This reminds me of the Greek myth of Persephone and Hades. Persephone is stolen down into the underworld by Hades. When her mother, Demeter, finally finds her and arranges her freedom, it is too late. Persephone has eaten four seeds during her stay. She is compelled to return four months out of every year for eternity. One month for each seed consumed, to reign as Queen of the Dead, because no one who has partaken of the Underworld can truly escape it. I've had a taste of this world, and like Cindy, I wonder if I'll always have a need to return.

I keep rewinding my conversation with Cindy as I drive back to Lompoc. I've lost track of how many times I've made this night trek home from the Havana Night Club. Cindy's words ring true. I think of the men I've met at the club. She's right. Some have told me that they've danced for ten or fifteen years, especially the older ones in their fifties and sixties. I can see how someone can get sucked into this lifestyle where every night is a carnival, and time passes like a thief. But who's to say that it's wrong? These guys seem genuinely happy. I wonder though. What happens when you can longer dance? Or when the hard times come? Do they feel lonely returning to an empty house night after night? Were they so tired from dancing that they neglected other areas of their life? My intuition tells me that everything has a price.

What about her warning about dating Esteban? If things don't work out between Esteban and I then I'd have to deal with seeing him with other women or stop dancing. Could I handle it? Is it worth the risk?

Yes, it is.

Given who I am, I have to take the chance. I don't believe in regrets. If I don't follow this path to wherever it leads I'll spend the rest of my life looking backwards. Knowing is better than not knowing.

The ghost of myself has been silent the whole ride home. To her, it's a no brainer. I wouldn't be following her out night after night if I was afraid to take on the unknown. If I was that kind of girl, she wouldn't waste her time with me. So, she sits by and lets me think through Cindy's words, as if my friend's cautions (although wise) would sway my decision. If the ghost of myself thought I needed any help, she'd lend it, but this time it isn't necessary. She knows I will chase her down. She's known this from the first time I turned the key to start my car late at night. So she relaxes and listens to the Salsa music, recalling all of my best dances of the evening, and thinks to herself, that girl has a long way to go before she dances like me.

Chapter 12 Esteban, The Dance Teacher

Saturday is finally here. My first Salsa lesson with Esteban. I've found a place for us to practice. We're meeting at the Lompoc Valley gym. The owner is very sweet and has agreed to let me use the aerobics room for our lesson. She's also letting Esteban in free of charge.

I don't have to wait long before I see his white Sentra enter the parking lot. I watch him through the tall glass windows that surround the front lobby. He's wearing a white t-shirt and jeans, very casual. I'm used to seeing him dressed up for a night of dancing. This is really happening. I can't believe it. I've wanted this since the first time I watched him dance.

"Hi," I walk over to him as he enters the doors.

"Hello," he gives me a hug and kiss on the cheek.

I introduce him to Tina who is working the front desk. She has him sign the waiver and the log book. I can see she's trying to tone down her smile. I'm sure all of my co-workers are going to hear about this. There will be rumors circulating around the gym by the time my lesson is over. I usher him away from the front desk and lead him over to where we'll be practicing.

"Here we are," I tell Esteban as I open the door. I can see he's surprised. It's a dancer's dream to practice in a large room with a shiny wooden floor and wall to wall mirrors. I love teaching my dance aerobics class in this room, but I love it even more when I dance in here alone.

"Do you have music? We can plug in your iPod or if you have CDs we can play those too," I point to the stereo system located in the front.

"I have music, but I want to teach you the Salsa basic without music first." He sounds more serious than what I'm used to with him. I've also noticed that he hasn't held my hand since his arrival.

"Okay," I put down my things and change into my dance shoes. He's ready to start, and I get the feeling this is going to be very business-like. I walk over and stand beside him facing the mirrors.

"First, we're going to practice the Salsa basic. We'll use the leader's basic, because that's what we use for teaching styling. You'll step forward with your left foot, come back together, step back with your right, and then back together again. The most important thing for you to practice is the counting. It's one, two, three, five, six, seven."

"What happened to four and eight?" I ask.

"That's the pause. You make a rock step forward and back to center on the one, two, three then pause on four, and then make a rock step to the back on counts five, six, seven and pause on eight," as Esteban explains this he moves with the counts to demonstrate how it flows together. I copy him watching us both in the mirror, trying my best to match his moves and timing.

"Your twisting too much, and I want your knees a little straighter. Also, you have to work on the pause," Esteban's directions unsettle me. He takes away everything I'm used to doing in my Latin dance classes. I feel like my flavor has been taken away and with it my rhythm.

"We're going to practice the basic with music," he tells me as he sets up his iPod.

The music fills the space. He joins me facing the mirror, and we start our basic. He makes it look easy. I'm having a rough time with it. I can follow him, but I have difficulty identifying the counts for myself.

We continue this for the entire song, which seems to be a really long one. Once it finishes, we keep going through the next song and the next. My mind wanders. Boredom creeps in. But the real problem? I keep losing the beat. This should be the easiest dance step I've ever done, but it's not. I mess up either with my feet or the timing. By the fifth song, I'm sweating not from exhaustion, but pure concentration. No matter how much I focus, I keep losing the basic. Esteban looks like he could do this for an hour. I'd bet money that he has, many times.

"I want you to practice your basic every day," Esteban has no smile on his face as he says this. I've realized this lesson will not be filled with laughter.

This is the pattern we follow for each new step. He teaches me twelve in all, twelve steps in three hours. I'm lucky to have been permitted bathroom breaks.

"The last thing I want to teach you today is how to move your arms," Esteban tells me. I look for traces of tiredness in him, but there is none. In the mirror, he looks the same as when we started. I, on the other hand, look like a mess. I'm worried I smell bad too. I've been sweating since the first hour.

"We're going to use the Cumbia step to practice the arm movements," he says as he starts moving his feet in a rock step pattern. I follow him. He steps with his right foot and does a rock step to the back with his left, and then he steps to the side with his left and does a rock step with his right foot. I notice that his body turns slightly with each step, as if it's just coming along for the ride. He then shows me a sequence of four arm movements that he layers on top of the footwork. Whatever my right arm does first, my left arm copies. My right arm swings across the body and the left follows. He scoops his right hand down and stretches it up straight overhead and I copy. He takes both hands and surrounds his head and lets them trace his body as he brings them down. I do the same. To finish, he sweeps both hands in front of his body as if he is gathering air. He plays the music, and we practice these moves nonstop. By the end, my shoulders are aching.

"Okay, that's it for today. I'm going to write these steps down for you. I want you to practice them every day. That's the only way you'll get better," Esteban grabs a paper and a pen. He creates my to-do list.

"I'm also going to give you some CD's that I want you to listen to as much as you can. You can practice counting the beats, so you can learn to hear it for yourself," Esteban hands me my list of steps and assigned listening music.

"We didn't get to practice dancing together," I tell him. I'm disappointed. I've been looking forward to dancing with him for a whole week now. I thought this would be my chance to ask questions and start figuring out how to follow the guy's hand signals. Dancing with a partner is a complete mystery to me, and I thought Esteban was going to start teaching me the secrets.

"You're not ready. I want you to learn this first. Next time, we can do some partner work. Trust me, you'll learn faster if you practice this exactly the way I showed you," as he says this it dawns on me that Esteban still hasn't smiled once throughout the entire lesson.

"Okay, I'll practice it every day," I promise him. My voice sounds flat in the open room. Esteban takes my hand in his as we move towards the door.

"Do you like ice cream?" Esteban asks, and there it is, the smile that's been absent.

"Yeah, but I haven't had any for a long time," I answer.

"I saw an ice cream shop that I want to take you to," Esteban shares with me as we walk out of the dance room.

"Sure, but let me clean up and change my clothes first." I am so grateful the gym has a shower. I look like a drowned rat (and probably smell like one too).

"Okay, I'll wait for you by the front desk." Esteban walks towards the lobby, and I rush into the Women's Locker Room. This will be the fastest shower ever. He will be alone out there with Tina and curious gym members who are eager for gossip. And who knows when Mike might show up?

When I finally walk over to Esteban, I see him standing there talking to Tina. I can only guess how much information she's sucked out of him. I can't miss the big smile on her face when she sees me coming.

Esteban drives us to the same shopping center we strolled around talking and holding hands during the last Salsa Night. He parks in front of a Mexican ice cream shop. I've never noticed it before, even though I must have passed by it many times.

Inside the shop there is an explosion of bright colors in various shades of pink, yellow and orange. I can see a variety of fresh fruit such as pineapple and strawberries being chopped on the counter. The glass display case houses the ice cream. It looks different from what I am used to seeing. The ice cream is on popsicle sticks and tucked inside are chunks of fresh fruit. Some are dusted with candy sprinkles or coconut shavings.

"They have fruit waters if you're thirsty. They're really good," Esteban informs me.

"I'd like to try one," I tell him. Given I've just been sweating for the last three hours, this sounds perfect.

"What flavor do you want?" He rattles off several names, most of which I don't recognize.

"Surprise me," seems like the most convenient answer.

Esteban chooses an ice cream popsicle with kiwi fruit tucked inside for himself and orders me a large agua de pina, a pineapple water.

I take one sip of my drink and wonder where it's been all my life. I'm not a fan of fruit juice, but this is amazing. I can taste the fresh pineapple. It is smooth and has a little sweetness without being overwhelming. I am in love.

"This is the best fruit drink I've ever had. Thank you," I tell Esteban. He smiles back. It's nice to see him smiling again. I've been missing it today.

"The ice cream here is better than any I've found in Oxnard. You're lucky to have this shop in Lompoc," Esteban shares with me as he finishes his first ice cream and goes back for a second. The man loves his ice cream. He must have inhaled it. I get the feeling this is the first of many ice cream dates.

"I like coming to Lompoc," Esteban tells me as he sits down with his ice cream popsicle filled with fresh strawberries. He gives me one of my favorite smiles. The one I see when he's doing crazy moves on the dance floor as I twirl around him.

"Really? You don't think it's boring?" I ask.

"No, I like the slower pace. I can relax. I'd like to visit you again next Saturday. What do you think?" He reaches across the table and gently holds my hand.

"Yes, I'd like that," I try to hide my smile, but I can't.

With Esteban, a new world opens up to me filled with different words, flavors, and passions. The ordinary transforms into the extraordinary like walking into the little Lompoc ice cream shop I've driven by a hundred times and tasting flavors I never imagined.

Chapter 13 Practice, Practice, Practice!

I practice every day. It's not easy. There are days I teach two dance aerobics classes. Practicing Salsa on top of two hours of intense cardio is brutal. I also lift weights and create new dance routines for my classes every week. Still, I'm not complaining. This is something I want.

The only private space I have is my bedroom. I'm incredibly lucky. My mother used to practice hula dancing in this room so it has hardwood floors and a mirror that spans most of one wall. The only piece of furniture is my daybed. My bedroom couldn't be better suited for me. I don't watch TV, so I'm glad there isn't one. I have a space to dance and sleep, and that's all I need.

I've downloaded Esteban's music to my iPod so I can practice early in the morning or late at night without bothering anyone. Typically, these are the only free hours I have to devote to Salsa. I'm committed to doing this, but I can't say that my heart is in it. I don't really like the steps he has given me to practice. It's so repetitive.

I always start with the basic. I do this for at least one song, if not two, and Esteban's songs are long, some last seven minutes. So, that is seven minutes of doing the same step over and over. If I'm honest, I find his music to be a little boring. I'm used to upbeat Salsa music like the types I use in my aerobics classes. The beat is obvious, and it has an energy you can't miss. This music isn't like that. The beat is subtle and sometimes hard to find. It has a smoother feel to it, and the singer doesn't always sound happy. Since I don't speak Spanish, I'm guessing that there is more depth to the lyrics in these songs and some are about lost love. But, that's not me. When I dance, I only feel one thing, happy.

I have to resist the urge to do other things. Sometimes, the music is so beautiful I want to express it with my body and just get lost in it. I start to add a little spin here and there, or a side to side step, and then remember Esteban was strict. When I practice the basic, I only do the basic, nothing else. He says that is the only way it will become natural for me. So, I go back to the basic. Then after a while, I want to do the basic my way, the way I feel it. I start to free my body more with accentuated twists of the hips and bend my knees more so there is more movement. Then I remember. Esteban said no. I need to twist less and not bend quite so deeply. Some bend of the knees, but not too much. Some movement of the hips, but not so crazy. I reign myself in, even if the music is tempting me to let go. I struggle against it. I practice all my steps the way he instructed me.

The next biggest challenge is the arm movements. Repeating the same four arm movements while keeping the Cumbia step going is mind numbing. I don't like it. My shoulders ache after the first couple of minutes. I shake them out and start again. The music tells my body to do something else, but I ignore it and stick to Esteban's instructions. According to him, repetition is the path to fluidity. If I want to move like him and have his speed, I have to practice like him.

At this point, when I have practiced all the steps on the to-do list, on the days I have energy leftover, I give myself the luxury of abandoning Esteban's rules. I let go. I let the music express whatever it wants to and allow it to flow like water through me. A place where there is no right or wrong, just expression. In the mirror, I can sometimes see it flow unhindered, but many times it gets stuck. It finds resistance either through overthinking or just an untrained body that is only learning how to dance. But it doesn't matter, because I just relax and try again. Those practices are bits of heaven on earth.

Chapter 14 Who Was That Guy?

"You look tired," Mike tells me as he approaches the front desk. It's not his usual greeting, but I guess he's right. I can feel it in my bones. I'm exhausted. It's closing time at the Lompoc Valley gym.

"Yeah, I do feel a little worn out tonight," I figure there's no point lying about it.

"Are your classes getting to you? I think you work in every gym in Lompoc, right?" Mike asks.

"Yep, but I love what I do. I have to work all these jobs or I'd never pay my bills. You know how it is in this industry. It's hard to make ends meet."

"I know, but you have to take care of yourself too. Is it the Salsa dancing? How often do you go out?"

"I go out about once a week, but sometimes I skip a week to catch up on sleep." I'm surprised he's asking so many questions. This isn't like him. I start my closing routine. I have to walk around the gym before locking up. Mike follows me.

I check every room, including the bathrooms, to make sure there are no members left in the building. My co-worker Tina is shutting down the computers. Mike doesn't usually hang out this late so it feels odd to have him with me.

"So, how is the dancing going?" Mike asks.

"I'm learning, but it's not easy. I'm having to change everything that comes naturally to me. It will take a lot of practice, but I'll get it," I answer as we head back to the front to turn out the lights and lock the lobby door.

Once outside Mike and I say goodnight to Tina, and he walks me to my car. Our cars are the only two left in the parking lot. Lompoc is a quiet town. Even though it's only nine o'clock, there is no one else around. Mike is handsome. There is no denying it. The moonlight creates a romantic back drop. I'm careful not to be seduced by it. He is my friend, my co-worker. But sometimes, at moments like these, when I find him so charming, I wonder why I've never wanted more. I lean back against my car as I chat with him.

"Don't worry about me. I'll be all right after a good night's sleep. Shouldn't we be more worried about you? Your boot camp class still starts at six in the morning, right? I think its past your bed time." I look him in the eye as I say this and smile.

"Yeah, I'm being reckless tonight. I'm just worried about you. I'm used to seeing you bubbling with energy, but ever since the last Salsa Night you seem to look more tired every day. What's up?" While saying this Mike's green eyes zero in on me for the last question. He's trying to read my reaction.

"Nothing really, it's just the same old routine. Like you said, I teach a lot of classes," I answer.

Mike looks downward as he continues on, "Tina said you had a Salsa lesson at the gym." After saying this, his eyes meet mine.

There it is, the motive for tonight's talk is revealed. Thanks, Tina.

"Yeah, I did. I found someone to teach me. I just had my first lesson with him."

"Did you find him at the club in Santa Barbara?" Mike asks.

"No, I met him here in Lompoc." I want to give as little information as possible. For some unknown reason, Mike seems curious.

"He lives in Lompoc?" Mike asks the question, but I'm guessing he already knows the answer. I bet Tina shared with him every detail she could about Esteban. There is no use trying to hide anything after all.

"No, he lives in Oxnard," I tell him.

"Was he at the last Salsa Night?" Mike keeps the questions coming. He's trying to narrow down the suspects. I figure the best way to end this interrogation is to volunteer the information he is looking for, otherwise we could be out here for a long time.

"Yeah, his name is Esteban. He was the one helping the Salsa instructor. He's a really good dancer, and he offered to teach me," I tell him.

"He came all the way from Oxnard to teach you Salsa?"

"Yes, he did."

"Hmmm," Mike pauses for a second and shifts his weight from foot to foot as he thinks, "I'm surprised."

"Why?" I ask.

"I would have thought that if someone was teaching you Salsa you would look happier. I would expect you to be bouncing around with excitement," Mike lets loose his observation and lets it take effect. He's right. I would have expected that too.

"It's just harder than I thought," I confess.

"How so?" Mike probes further.

"It's like I have to reverse everything I would do naturally. I can't be free to do what I want. If I want to bend my knees I have to straighten them more. If I want to twist my hips, I have to tone it down. And then there is this pause in the middle of the Salsa basic that just feels weird like I'm a robot. It doesn't feel smooth. The way I practice is so repetitive. It drives me crazy," I let it all out. I surprise myself by how easily my complaints jump out of my mouth, as if they've been running around in my head like flies trapped in a house.

"Let me see that move, the Salsa basic," Mike stands back with his hands on his hips, boot camp-style.

"No way, I'm not doing it."

"Let me see it so I understand."

"No."

"We could stay here all night or you can show it to me," Mike smiles to take the edge off his words, but I can feel he means it.

"Ok," I give in because I'm tired and want to go home.

"I want you to do it the way Esteban taught you, not how you would do it naturally," he tells me.

"Ok," I take a breath before I start. I count the steps aloud as I move, "one, two, three...five, six, seven." I do the Salsa basic as best as I can. I try not to twist too much and hold the pause in the correct place.

"Keep going," Mike instructs.

I follow his instructions even though it feels awkward. I'm used to my body feeling loose, but dancing this way makes me feel stiff. I eventually stop unable to bare it any longer.

"It doesn't look like you," Mike announces. "I've seen you teach your dance classes, and I can barely recognize you."

"I know. That's what it feels like." Even though I know he's right, I feel crushed. I've practiced so hard this week trying to make it look smooth and natural.

"Do you think it's because you're tired?" Mike tries to make sense of it.

"It could be. I've been practicing this a lot. I feel exhausted," I let my guard down and the truth comes spilling out.

"I know you want to learn to dance, but what's the rush? You seem almost stressed about it. Dancing is supposed to be fun, right?"

"Yes, but I want to impress Esteban. He is such a good dancer. I want him to be proud of my progress so he keeps teaching me. I get the feeling Esteban takes dancing very seriously," being tired makes me say more than I want to. I regret the words as soon as they fly out of my mouth. I wish I could stuff them back in.

"Why do you think that?" Mike asks.

"It's strange. He never smiled once during our lesson. We practiced for three hours and not one smile. He is business-like when it comes to dancing, no laughing, no joking. He wants to start his own dance company with the best dancers. Esteban is different away from the practices. He's fun to be around. He changes when he teaches."

"A dance company, huh? Well, that would explain a lot," Mike answers.

"Do you think so?"

"Yes."

"How?" Now I'm the one asking the questions.

"You two are dancing for different reasons. That's why you're stressed out and tired," Mike relaxes his shoulders and arms from his boot camp stance. "Esteban wants to build a dance company. He's going for perfection. That's why he doesn't smile during the lesson. You, on the other hand, dance because it makes you feel good. You love it. When you teach your dance classes you can't stop smiling. It makes you happy. You're miserable because you're trying to be something you're not," Mike finishes his assessment.

"Miserable is a strong word. I'm not miserable. I just want to learn how to dance and it's going to take practice to learn it the right way. It just doesn't feel natural yet, that's all," I'm not going to let him discourage me.

"That's true. Learning it the right way does take practice, and it's not going to look good for a while. That's normal. But, that's not what I'm talking about. You have a lightheartedness about the way you dance. It makes you so happy anyone can see it, and it practically makes you float around the gym the rest of the day. This pressure you're putting yourself under is stealing that away, and it doesn't have to be that way." Mike is usually the first one to say keep going when times are tough, but tonight his advice is like a giant stop sign.

"You don't understand. This is what I want. I feel really lucky to have this opportunity." I'm not giving up, I tell myself.

"Ok, let me put it this way. How old are you?"

"Forty," I tell him.

"You've spent the last twenty years taking care of your kids and husband, right?"

"Yes"

"How long do you think you will be able to go out dancing the way you do?"

"I don't know, but I want to do it for as long as I can."

"My point is this. Life is short. You've spent so much time taking care of others. Right now, you're still young and beautiful. You have the opportunity to live a little, but it won't last forever. Take it. Make the most of it. If you want to learn to dance, then do it. But, don't let anything steal your smile. Don't waste this time being stressed out and tired. Besides, I can't have my Amazing Scarlet looking grumpy at the gym all the time," with this his green eyes soften and his smile turns broad. I know he wants me to be happy.

"I'll think about what you've said. I'm still going to take the lessons, because this is what I want. But, I will consider everything you've told me," I answer. The truth is I will. "Thank you," I tell Mike as I open my car door. I resist the urge to hug him. I need to keep the boundary between us, especially in the moonlight.

"Goodnight, Scarlet," Mike answers.

"Goodnight. See you tomorrow. Good luck at 6 a.m.,' and with that we go our separate ways.

The ghost of myself considers everything Mike has to say. He is a smart man. His words make a lot of sense, and he knows me so well. But, he may not be entirely right in this case. Growth requires stretching beyond and sometimes it's a messy process. The path isn't always linear, especially if you don't know exactly where your headed, and if you always travel in a straight line you might miss out on the lessons given on the detours. Beginnings are not always perfect, but they are at least that, a beginning. I like what he said about the smile. I think it's better that I bury that for now like a hidden treasure that waits to be found at the correct time. Dancing with Esteban, practicing these steps, this is where she needs to be to get to where we're going.

Chapter 15 Did You Practice?

Today is the day. I'm waiting for Esteban to arrive for our second Salsa lesson. I have mixed feelings. I'm excited to see him, but I'm worried. I've practiced as much as I can, but it doesn't feel like it's enough. Despite my hard work, I don't see much improvement. In my mind, I know the steps by heart, but unfortunately my body doesn't seem able to match the pretty picture in my head. I try to ignore these thoughts and instead think about how much I've been waiting to see Esteban again.

He still calls me almost every night. Sometimes we talk on the phone for ten minutes, other times the conversation lasts until one in the morning. I never get bored talking to him. He shares with me his goals and dreams and asks me to share mine in return. So even though he lives an hour and a half away, I feel like he is a part of my everyday life.

Finally, I see his car pull into the gym parking lot. I'm waiting outside this time so I can avoid hanging out at the front desk with Tina. My plan is to get Esteban passed her as quickly as possible.

"Hello," I greet him as he hops out of his car. He's wearing a black t-shirt, jeans and a pair of sunglasses.

"Hello," he answers as he gives me a hug and kiss.

"How was the drive?"

"Good. I hit a little traffic in Santa Barbara, but after that it was easy," Esteban shares as he reaches into his car for his music and dance shoes.

Tina is away from her desk as we enter the gym. I have Esteban sign the guest log, and we make our way to the aerobics room.

"How are your dance practices going in Oxnard?" I ask.

"They're going good. The guys are consistent, but the girls don't always show up. I have one girl who is a natural dancer though. She catches on fast," he tells me as we open the doors to the dance area.

"What's her name?"

"Melinda. She's been coming to the practices for the past two weeks. She's already a good dancer. I can tell she loves to dance," he shares. I feel my heart sink in my chest.

"Have you been practicing?" Esteban asks as we set up the music and get ready to start.

"Yes, but I still don't seem to have the hang of it," I give him the truth.

"Let me see you do the basic by yourself," he tells me as he starts the music.

Please be a song I can hear the counts clearly, a little voice pleads inside my head.

The music begins, and of course, it's one of his confusing songs. I listen carefully. I try to relax my body to let the music flow through me. This is how I stay on time when I teach my aerobic classes. But as soon as I start to do this, even though I've found the beat, I can see Esteban looking at me disapprovingly. I've resorted to my old ways of twisting too much and bending too deeply. Esteban stops the music.

"Remember to keep your legs a little straighter, and don't twist as much. If you twist too much while we dance together, it will be harder for us to do the combinations. The legs need to be straighter so you look more elegant. Try again," with these words he starts the music back up. He didn't raise his voice, but the strictness in his tone bothers me. He can't see how hard I've been trying.

I do as he says. I tone down the twisting, bend less, and remember the pause. However, as soon as I do this my body stiffens and loses the ability to feel the beats. I'm left to just listening for the counts which at times is obvious enough for me to catch, but other times slips away when the singer's voice blocks out the instruments. Without a kinesthetic awareness of the music, I feel lost in a sea of sound. Esteban stops the music again.

"Trying counting it out loud," he instructs me. He plays the music again. He starts me off with the counting, and I continue it on. It helps. I'm able to keep the beat, but when I look in the mirror it is exactly as Mike says. I can't recognize myself. It's as if the life is drained out of my dancing. I know I am capable of so much more.

Esteban joins in with me, and with him as a leader I don't have to worry about losing the counts. I just follow. Sometimes, I wonder if he is off beat though. There are times I hear it differently. Not noticeably different, but a subtle resistance to how I feel the music wants to flow through me. Since I'm a beginner struggling to learn to identify the counts for myself, I can't be sure. At the end of the song, Esteban stops the music and turns towards me. He's not smiling.

"You didn't practice, did you?" His words sting my eyes. I steady myself so I won't cry.

"I told you the truth. I did. I don't know why I'm having a hard time getting this, but I did practice," I answer.

"If you practiced, I'd be able to see it," Esteban starts to pack away the music. "Why don't we do something else? Let me take you out to lunch. I haven't had anything to eat yet," he offers.

"I was hoping you could teach me how to dance with you," I throw it out there, what I really want.

"You're not ready. If you want to learn to dance with a partner, you have to learn the basic first. Otherwise, you'll never dance good. You have to practice," his voice is flat.

The rest of the date was a blur. I was there, but not really. He took me to lunch and a movie. I was too sad to enjoy myself. I pretended not to be wounded. I don't know why. I guess I was afraid that if I tried to share my feelings I wouldn't be able to hold back the tears. He didn't mention anything more about the dancing. I didn't either.

Chapter 16 The Cumbia King

I still practice. I don't care what Esteban or anyone else thinks. I'm doing this. Since his method isn't working for me I'm making some adjustments.

I begin my practice with the Salsa basic, but I'm not so worried about being on the correct beat. Instead, I relax. I try my best to find it when I can and keep going when I lose it. I don't stop until the song ends. I figure one day I'll get it. After the basic, I do the arm movements with the Cumbia step for one song, and only one song. As for the rest of the steps, I rotate which ones I practice so I'm not having to go through all of them every time. These changes leave adequate time and energy to practice the regimen I've created for myself.

Esteban won't practice dancing with me, and I only get to dance with partners once week at the Havana Night Club. From what I've seen, there are three main steps that are used over and over in partner dancing. They are the basic, right-hand turn, and cross body lead. Most of the combinations are based on those three steps or variations of them. If I can dance those on my own, then I don't have to rely on a partner to keep my balance. If those three steps are automatic, I can focus my attention on other things like reading the hand signals or adding styling moves. So for four songs, I practice these steps in order. When I get dizzy, I just keep repeating the basic until I'm ready to try again. I pick various tempos usually starting with slow songs and then trying faster ones.

For the last couple of songs, I am free to improvise. I think of it as "unconventional" Salsa. Any dance moves I can come up with is fair game. The last thing I want to do is look like a robot, and my goal is not to look like everyone else. I want to look like me, good or bad. To do that, I have to feel the music for myself. I need to connect with it not just with my feet or my arms, but my entire body. The music should be able to express itself with whatever body part it wants. I can't do that if I'm stiff and robotic.

Esteban calls me every night. I haven't shared with him how hurt I was over the last lesson, and he has never asked me if I'm practicing. He shares with me how his dance group is progressing, and unfortunately, how well Melinda is doing. They've started hitting the dance clubs as a group, and I get to hear how everyone compliments him on his new student. I can't say that it feels great hearing these adventures, but I try to be supportive. I know he is working towards his dream, and he encourages me as I work towards my Personal Trainer certification. I invited him to go with me to the Havana Night Club tonight, but he said he couldn't. He told me his dance group goes to the 805 Club in Oxnard on Thursdays.

I reasoned that either I could stay at home consoling myself with a gallon of chocolate ice cream while another girl lives out my dream of dancing with Esteban or I could get in my car and head to the Havana Night Club.

I wrestle with my feelings on my drive there. It's so unfair I could scream, but of course, I don't. I resist the urge to beat up on myself with those thoughts of what's wrong with me and why couldn't I just catch on to that stupid basic. I imagine Melinda being everything I'm not. I know she is young and in her early twenties. As the Salsa music plays in my car, I can envision her twirling about Esteban effortlessly with perfect timing and styling that rivals my friend Cindy. The onlookers watch in amazement. Afterwards, the Salseros line up to pat Esteban on the back and congratulate him on his beautiful student. My imagination can be very cruel.

I am, however, aware of another undercurrent of emotions that rides alongside the waves of jealousy. It's a quiet knowing of sorts, a resolution. The determined part of me that says Melinda doesn't really matter one bit. I am going to do what I have set out to do, even if I have to do it alone.

97

The drive goes quickly with my mind preoccupied with unwanted thoughts, and I find myself once again walking through the open doors of the Havana Night Club. As soon as I hear the music, I know I've made the right choice. The dance floor is alive with people whirling around each other. I can feel the energy and the tug to join in. Here, life is a carnival.

My friend Rick suddenly appears, takes my hand, and guides me into the frenzy. I am immersed in the party. My bad mood is gone. How can I be upset with Rick's big grin shining down on me? He surprises me with new moves, and although I've never encountered them before I can follow because Rick gives such a clear lead. It's easy to figure out where he wants me to go, and what he wants me to do. His body is much looser this time. He shakes his shoulders and adds more spins of his own. It finally dawns on me. He's been holding back. Practicing the basic, cross body lead and right-hand turn on my own has paid off. I am steadier on my feet, and now Rick can do more with me. He is a much better dancer than I had imagined. I wonder how much more of this Salsa world will open up to me as I keep improving.

Rick is only the first in a string of dances. There are three gentlemen here tonight that I dance with every time I visit this club. From what I've seen, these three gentlemen make sure no woman spends the night as a wall flower. I've seen them dance with all the girls, especially those who are not asked by anyone else. If I'm standing by myself watching for more than one dance, one of these fellows are sure to invite me on the dance floor. All three are good dancers. This is a rarity in the Salsa world. Most skilled leaders avoid taking partners on the dance floor who are not good followers. There is a saying in the Salsa world that anything that goes wrong on the dance floor is the man's fault. If the woman messes up, it's the guy's fault. If she runs into someone, dances offbeat, falls down, or gets her foot stabbed by the 4-inch heel of the woman next to her, blame the leader. Since the good dancers are busy trying to out dance each other, one need only guess why they pick the best dancers for partners. These three gentlemen break that rule, and the Havana Night Club is a better place for it.

Half of the night goes by before I step outside for my first break. I stand by the outdoor fireplace. The stars shine down on me, and I can't believe I'm here. It's approaching midnight, and I'm in Santa Barbara underneath this beautiful sky doing what I love, dancing. I'm so glad I came tonight. This is the first time I've felt like I'm getting it. I'm starting to hold my own on the dance floor.

"Hello, dancing queen," Cindy calls out behind me. I turn around to see my friend, and of course, she's beautiful as ever. Tonight, she is wearing a pink dress with a short hemline. Her hair is let loose in long curls that fall to her mid-back.

"Hello, beautiful," I give her a hug.

"I see you've been dancing non-stop as usual," Cindy stands with me by the fire.

"I'm guessing you have too," I answer.

"Always," she smiles.

"Going solo again tonight, huh? How are things with Esteban?"

"We're doing okay," I regret the words as soon as I hear them out loud. My voice sounds flat. I should have tried to sound more excited. After all, we just started dating. Cindy is sure to pick up on it and ask questions.

"And," she pauses, "how are the lessons?"

"It's a lot of hard work," I laugh. If I joke around it will be easier to change the subject. I don't feel like talking about Esteban tonight.

"I saw him at La Pura Vida last week," Cindy adds. "I think he was there with a group of his students. I've seen them together at a few of the clubs lately."

"Yeah, he told me that. They've been out dancing a lot."

"There are three guys, and one girl that I keep seeing with him," Cindy tells me this and her voice grows softer and timid. I don't like where this is going.

"That would be Melinda. He told me about her," I figure if I let Cindy know that I am already aware of Melinda she won't feel the need to tell me anything more.

"This is hard for me to say, but I'm going to say it. He was dancing with her a lot. I don't like it. I just don't want you to be surprised," Cindy looks like she wants to cry. Watching her eyes tear up makes me feel like crying too, but I hold it together.

"Don't worry about me. I don't know what will happen between me and Esteban. I have a lot of respect for him and imagine that whatever happens we will end up as friends. As for Melinda? He tells me she's just his student. I guess time will tell, but either way, I'll be okay," as I finish a man walks up to Cindy and asks her for a dance. I am so grateful for the interruption. I give her a smile, and she accepts his invitation.

I'm shell-shocked. I find myself wandering around the courtyard. I don't want to go back to the Salsa dance floor. I want to keep my distance from Cindy. Also, I'm feeling beat up by Salsa. The men are trying so hard to out dance each other. Esteban is dancing with another girl tonight instead of me because he wants to be the best. Mike is right. This isn't me. I love Salsa, but all of this other crap that goes with it is exhausting. What happened? Where did I take the wrong turn? How did everything get so screwed up?

I walk towards the Cumbia dance floor because it's the farthest I can travel from the Salsa area and still be in the club. I find a spot to stand and watch. As sad as I feel, watching the dancers makes me feel a little better. These people know how to have a good time. Anything goes on this dance floor. The men have bigger smiles, which I suspect is heavily alcohol-induced. Nothing is going to bother them. What's missing on this dance floor? Crazy dips, body rolls, aerial stunts, and the dramatic poses that are often seen in Salsa are absent here, along with the egos that inspire them. Instead, it's just people feeling the music and having fun. If only I could take this vibe with me when I dance Salsa. Then I would be home.

A man breaks my trance. He has a nice smile and a bald head. His clothes are simple. He has a loose fitted white long sleeve shirt and jeans. He offers his hand, and I accept the invitation.

He feels at ease on the dance floor. He is a smooth dancer so it feels like we're gliding through the steps. I know most of the basic combinations from dancing with Esteban so he doesn't hesitate to start spinning me around him. My worries float away from me. I hear the guy next to me singing to his partner. My guy isn't singing, but it wouldn't surprise me if he did.

My partner slows me down to show me something new. He steps forward with his left foot and signals me to step forward with my right to match him. He taps his right foot behind his left and steps back to the starting position. I mirror him. He then does the same sequence starting with his right foot, and I copy him starting with my left. We are mirroring each other as we practice the combination slowly so I can get it. Then he signals a change. Instead of doing a tap on the floor, he wants me to lift my back foot up and wrap it around my standing leg so we can tap our shoes together. Again, we practice this slowly until I get a good grasp of it. Finally, he picks up speed. It's amazing. I can do it!

He lets loose his hips to add a twist to the movement, and I let loose too. He then resumes the dance with the spins and usual Cumbia steps, but frequently adds our new combination so I can practice. I love it. We're twisting and tapping our shoes together. I've learned this painlessly. I had fun the whole time. Mike is right. Not all learning has to be misery. There is another way.

I follow a pattern for the rest of the night. I brave the Salsa floor until I get frustrated trying to be perfect. Then I cross the room to the Cumbia floor. The Cumbia King is always there waiting to take me back out to learn more. Each new move he breaks down slowly, so I am never overwhelmed. And so the night goes, until the club closes. By the early morning hours, he has introduced me to more steps than I can remember. The strangest part? I don't recall the Cumbia King ever talking to me. He taught me all of this without saying a word. I don't even know his real name.

Chapter 17 Don't You Dare Give Up

"You look like you're working hard," Angie's voice wakes me up from my books. I see that sweet smile of hers looking down at me.

"I am. I like to study here at the Coffee House, so if I fall asleep someone will wake me up." It's true. I'm so tired at night I fall asleep while studying at home. "Have a seat. I need a study break. So how have you been?" I ask.

"Everything is fine. Busy as usual, but I want to hear about you and this new guy. What's his name again?" Angie takes a seat and leans in closer. Her eyes are fixed on me as she starts her questions.

"Esteban," I answer.

"Oh, I like that name. It sounds very sexy, especially for a dancer. Are you two still dating? He was going to give you a lesson, right?"

"Yes, and he did give me a lesson. Actually, two lessons," I add.

"How did it go?"

"Not so great."

"Really? What happened?" Angie's eyes change from sparkling with happiness to utter despair. She's an emotional barometer that seems to register my every mood.

"As hard as I tried, I couldn't catch on quick enough, and he stopped teaching me. He thought I wasn't practicing, but the tragic part is that I practiced my heart out. I was just so awful he couldn't tell."

"That's terrible. I'm sorry," she pauses before continuing on, "It doesn't make any sense, though. You can dance. Most of Lompoc knows that. Is he just being hard on you?"

"I don't know, but that's not the worst part. He has another student named Melinda, and I have to hear how wonderful she is all the time. He takes her out dancing everywhere to show her off. It's really depressing."

"You're still dating?"

"Yes," I answer.

"Why?" Angie looks confused.

"Well, besides the dancing being screwed up, I really like him. He calls me every night, and outside of dancing we have a good time."

"He calls you every night?" Angie asks.

"Yes, we talk to each other for hours. He actually cares about my day. I've never had that before. Whenever I have a problem at work, he listens and gives me ideas."

"That sounds pretty nice."

"It is. All day long I take care of people. It's nice having someone ask me how I'm doing. I don't feel so alone." I hear the emotion rising in my voice. I take a breath. "It's just the damn dancing thing. I wish I knew how to fix it."

"Have you told him how you feel?"

"No"

"Why not?"

"I can't seem to get the words out. I'm afraid I'll start crying. You know when my husband first left me I cried horribly for days. Since then, no matter how awful I've felt at times, I don't cry. Every time I start to tell Esteban how important this is to me, I can feel the tears ready to spill out, and I hate it."

"I know, but if you want to stay with him you're going to have to tell him how you feel. Give him a chance to change things. He can't read your mind. If you cry then you cry, but at least you'll start standing up for yourself. Besides, you're beautiful. He's an idiot if he doesn't want to take you out dancing all the time to show you off," Angie smiles. This is why I love Angie. Her words do battle against the self-doubt I've had beating me up in my head.

"Okay, I will," I promise.

"You haven't stopped dancing, have you?"

"No, in fact, I went out a couple of nights ago," I can already hear a difference in my voice. It sounds lighter and more playful.

"Good. Don't you dare stop dancing!" Angie glares at me and then starts laughing which gets me started. No one else would find this funny, but her and I find any excuse to laugh together. "Tell me about your night out."

"I met the Cumbia King," I begin as we settle in with our coffee, and I give every detail of my last adventure.

Chapter 18 A New Perspective

This evening we're having another Salsa Night in Lompoc. I'm dressed up and ready to enter the club. Well, almost. I can't get myself out of the car. Esteban and I talked last night. He told me he's bringing all of his students to Lompoc, including Melinda. So, even though I love to dance, I find myself sitting in my car with my seat belt on.

"Oh, I don't think so." I can imagine the ghost of myself sitting in the passenger's seat with her arms crossed annoyed with me. "There is no way Esteban is coming to Lompoc with this Melinda girl, and you're left sitting in the car. I know you're not going to let that happen." She sighs. Then something catches her eye, "Oh, would you look at that? If you can pull yourself out of that weird funk you're in and check out who's here, you might be surprised."

I see Mike entering the club along with Pablo. Both men are gorgeous as always. One dark-haired and handsome, the other sandy blonde and dreamy.

"Oh, yes," I think back to the ghost of myself sitting next to me, "this might help." The seat belt is unbuckled and in I go.

I follow them into the club hoping to catch up with them when someone else steals my attention. Esteban is sitting at a table with his students eating dinner. A young woman with chin-length brown hair is seated next to him laughing. I guess I wasn't invited. Unfortunately, he notices me and walks over. If I could snap my fingers and disappear I would, but since I can't I remind myself to breathe and stay calm.

"Hi," Esteban says as he gives me a hug and kiss on the cheek.

"Hi, I didn't know you were going to have dinner before the lesson," I tell him. I'm going to take Angie's advice and be direct. This relationship is not going the way I want. Why wouldn't he think to invite me? I haven't seen him for two weeks. I ask him out dancing, and he doesn't go. He finally comes to Lompoc and has dinner with his friends and doesn't even think about asking me to join. Really? Did he even miss me? This girl is sitting next to him when he comes to my little Lompoc, dancing with him at the clubs, and it isn't a stretch of the imagination to think I will be watching them dance together the entire night. Enough already!

"Yeah, we were hungry so we thought we'd order some food. How have you been?" He asks.

"Fine." Okay, I'm back to lying, but that's so I don't have a complete melt down. I don't want to overreact. He stands there awkwardly not saying much. Is he even going to invite me over?

"Do you see any of your friends here?" Esteban breaks the silence.

"Yeah," I answer. He hasn't asked me over to his table. We keep standing in the middle of the restaurant while people walk around us. "Are you done eating?" I ask.

"No, we just got our food," he answers. I keep having to move out of the way for the waiters to pass by. He looks over to his table, but doesn't move towards it. "If you want to say hi to your friends, it's okay. I'll head back over to my table," he tells me. So, he's not going to invite me over.

"Sure, since it seems your table doesn't have room for me," I answer and walk off. If he tried to say anything else, I didn't hear. I make a bee-line for the Ladies Room.

I am not going to cry. Whenever I get frustrated or angry, I have a nasty habit of wanting to cry. Instead of yelling, tears spill out. I hate it. I am not going to do that here. I pull myself together. No one else is in the bathroom. Breathe. Count to ten. Relax. So what? I tell myself. What does it matter? Why is this upsetting me so much? I could pick so many other things in my life to be crying about. My divorce, poverty, sons growing up in a broken home, living with my parents, losing my house, the list is long. Why this? What's wrong with me? Why is learning to dance so important, and why am I with this guy? My life makes no sense, and I am being ridiculous.

Two women enter the bathroom. It shakes me out of my thoughts. I leave before they can tell I'm upset. I take one more deep breath and re-enter the club. I don't have to travel far before I see Mike and Pablo.

"Hello, you two," I manage a quick smile and give both guys a hug.

"Hello, Scarlet. You look beautiful tonight," Pablo says as he gives me a kiss on the cheek.

"I can't believe you're here again. I thought there was no way you'd ever come back," I tease Mike.

'I'm kind of surprised myself, but Pablo was visiting and there's nothing else to do in Lompoc on a Saturday night. So, here I am," Mike answers. I don't believe him. He's not looking me in the eye. "I guess you're ready to dance. It looks like Esteban is here. Are you sitting at his table?" Mike asks.

"No, I guess I'm on my own. Can I hang out with you guys?" I try to make my voice sound carefree, but inside I feel pathetic. Mike is staring at me. I can tell he's trying to read how I'm feeling.

"Mike tells me you've been taking lessons. How are they going?" Pablo asks the one question I'd like to avoid.

"They're not. Esteban stopped teaching me. I couldn't catch on fast enough. I tried. I practiced, but I was so bad that he thought I wasn't serious," I tell the truth but I can't look at their faces while I say it.

"You haven't given up, have you?" Mike asks.

"Of course, not. I went out dancing a couple of nights ago, and I practice every day on my own. It's just hard to learn to dance with a partner when I have no one to practice with."

"Well, I'm here," Pablo offers his hand. "Let's see what I can help you with," he gently guides me to the dance floor.

The deejay is setting up the sound system, and the dance floor is empty. There are a few people standing around waiting, but most are seated at the tables having dinner. Pablo and I are in our own little world.

He takes my hands and starts to lead me while he counts out loud, "one, two, three…five, six, seven." We start with a few basics, right-hand turns and a cross body lead, which I can easily follow.

"Nice! You've improved a lot since I last danced with you," he tells me. "Let me show you something that will help you with following." We stop and he holds my hands in front of him, "I want you to only give me the weight of your hands, no more and no less. Don't grip my hands, I don't want you to back lead. Right now, you have an idea of what comes next because the moves are simple, but when you dance with a good partner he will surprise you with moves you wouldn't expect. I want you to be a blank slate. That way you can react quickly. When you spin make a tiny hook of your fingers like this so I have something to hold on to, but again only give me the weight of your hands and nothing more, okay?" His voice is comforting and I feel my hands relax in his. "Yes, just like that. This is how your hands should feel in mine," Pablo smiles.

He starts to lead, and I follow. I can feel the difference. By simply placing the weight of my hands in his I become more sensitive to reading the signals. He can maneuver me easier. I can spin faster without friction slowing me down. He spins me twice, and I find it easy. He then throws in a triple spin and I can do it. He stops.

"You have natural speed, Scarlet. Not a lot of dancers do," he smiles. I can't control the goofy grin on my face. This is the first compliment I've been given by a Salsero. Learning doesn't feel so hopeless. The deejay starts up a Salsa song.

Pablo lets loose. He plays with the music shaking his shoulders and adding footwork, but he never loses his ability to lead. I feel confident that he will place me wherever he wants. With my body relaxed, I feel the music pulse through me. He starts throwing in double spins and triple spins, and at times, he sets me free to dance on my own. I love watching him freestyle and when he is done, he asks for my hands again so we can dance together. By the end of the song, I am slightly out of breath, but I feel happy.

I notice a crowd of people surrounding the dance floor. Esteban and Melinda are among the onlookers. How long have they been watching? Pablo senses my embarrassment and leads me over to the bar to get a drink.

"I can see that dancing makes you happy," Pablo tells me as he hands me a bottled water.

"Yes, I can think of few things that make me feel more alive," I share.

"Then don't give up. If you ever need help learning just give me a call, okay?" Pablo walks us back over to Mike.

"You two had a crowd of admirers," Mike announces as we stand by him. I see Esteban trying to catch my eye, but I avoid looking in his direction. I wonder what he thought of my dancing. He starts to move towards me, but Suzy interrupts.

"If you're here for the Salsa lesson make your way to the dance floor. We're getting started," she announces.

For the first half of the lesson we dance solo learning a short choreography that we can take home and practice. I glance occasionally at Melinda. I don't get it. From what I see, Melinda is not a good dancer. She's not bad either. The word that comes to mind is boring. She is a boring dancer. Nothing compels you to watch her. Her steps are done correctly, but they are executed sloppily. There is no flavor. She is a pretty girl, but again like her dancing, nothing captures the attention. I feel guilty sizing her up like this. I wouldn't normally be this critical, but to hear Esteban talk I would have expected so much more. Instead, I'm confused. What does he see in her dancing? Do I really dance worse than this? Instead of feeling jealous, I am baffled.

Suzy announces a break before the second half of the lesson which will be partner work. I decide to sneak out of the restaurant while they teach this part. I don't feel like talking to Esteban, and there will be no avoiding him during the lesson. Luckily, no one sees me leave.

When I return, the lesson has ended. I see out-of-towners, dancers from Santa Barbara. I say hi and give them a hug as I make my way over to the dance floor.

"So, there you are," I hear Esteban's voice as he walks up beside me. Before I can say anything, he takes my hand and leads me out for a dance.

I remember why I love dancing with him. He keeps me in motion and guessing at his every move. I react faster this time. I have no time to think. I am immersed in the moment. Esteban is all around me and his hands speak to me showing me new ways to feel the music. It's his speed I miss when I dance with other men. Every part of me feels alive and present. We dance song after song until Esteban finally stops us.

"Scarlet, I'm going to dance this one with Melinda," he tells me. "There are dancers here from Santa Barbara, and this is a good song. This is the kind of song where the teachers show they can dance." Esteban's words do not hit me well. I let his hands go and walk off.

I leave the club and stand outside. The night air has a slight chill, and I'm hoping it will cool my temper. So far, it hasn't. I could peek in the windows beside me to watch Esteban and Melinda dance, but I'm not tempted. I'd rather not.

"You're a better dancer than her," I hear a voice call out as it moves towards me. I turn around to find Pablo joining me.

"Who?" I ask.

"That girl Esteban is dancing with right now. I'm guessing she's his star student and that you are his girlfriend," Pablo smiles.

"What makes you think that?"

"Well, it's a little obvious. Esteban stares at you all the time, especially when he sees you with me. Just now it looks like he said something you didn't like and you're here outside instead of dancing. And that girl he's dancing with knows his combinations, but doesn't have a clue how to dance with anyone else. I know. I tried dancing with her," he softens his voice and leans against the building. "Ah, Scarlet, dating a teacher is never easy, especially one that teaches women how to dance."

"I thought it would be different," I confess. "You don't think she's a better dancer than me?"

"Not even close," he answers.

"Why?" I ask.

"A few reasons, but the first one that comes to mind is that she doesn't love it like you do," as Pablo says this he relaxes his body and puts his hands in his pockets.

"How can you tell?"

"You come alive when you dance. I can see it in your eyes and the way you can't stop smiling. Whether you know what to do or not, you try your hardest. Your partner has your full attention as if no one else exists. Also, the amount of improvement you've made in such a short amount of time tells me you practice every day. I love to dance too. I guess that's why I recognize it in someone else when I see it," he finishes his words and looks up at the night sky.

"Esteban doesn't see it," I answer back.

"That's because he wants you to dance like that girl, and you can't do that. You're not a robot," Pablo gives a few robotic moves with his arms and hands. I can't help but laugh. "You have your own style. Yes, you have to learn the steps better and practice, but I can tell you have ideas you want to explore and steps you want to create. I'm guessing you don't want to look like everyone else, right?"

"How do you know this?"

"Because if you wanted to look like everyone else, I'm sure you would. It isn't that hard, especially when you're determined. You dance differently, because you feel it differently. If you give up how the music makes you feel, then there would be no point in dancing at all. And," he pauses, "I would have no fun dancing with you," with these last words he looks me in the eye.

"I wish Esteban felt that way. That girl's name is Melinda. He stopped dancing with me to dance with her. He said that it was a good song, and he wanted to show off with her," as I say the words I look at the ground.

"That's only because she knows his combinations. Like I said, she doesn't dance well with anyone else. She's too dependent on him, and that makes you the better dancer."

"I don't understand," I look up at him.

"What makes a good dancer is the ability to dance with anyone, regardless of their level or style. In your case, the ability to follow any leader. You're learning the hard way, by dancing with lots of men. It's teaching you to be adaptable, and how to connect with a variety of people. To Esteban, Melinda seems to be the better dancer because she knows his combinations. It's all she practices. But in the long run, relying on only him and not herself will be a weakness. You are on the right track. Every time you go out dancing by yourself you're being exposed to new combinations and ideas. Dancing with everyone will make you a stronger dancer. Trust me," Pablo pulls himself away from the wall and starts to go back in.

"Pablo?" I call out to him.

"Yes," he answers.

I walk over to him and hug him, "Thank you."

"Any time, Scarlet. See you in there," he flashes one of those smiles I love and passes through the doors. I pause a moment to let his words sink in. They feel good. My ear catches a change in the music. Cumbia. I hear a Cumbia song. I go back in the club hoping to find someone to dance with.

As soon as I walk through the door a man steps forward and asks me to dance. I recognize him. I've seen him at the Havana Night Club. I might have danced with him before, but I'm not sure. He is only a little taller than me. I'm guessing he's about a decade older judging by his silver hair and beer belly. I take his hand, and we head towards the music.

There are less dancers on the floor. Most of the Salsa dancers are taking a break while some Cumbia dancers venture over from the bar for the first time tonight. The guys in Esteban's group are hanging around watching. Melinda is on the sidelines too. Esteban is standing next to her.

It's a wild ride. My partner grips my hands a little firmer than what I'm used to, but I've learned to expect that with Cumbia. He has me spinning around him at lightning speed. He throws in the steps that the Cumbia King taught me like tapping our feet together. He also shows me new moves like bringing me close to him and then having me duck under his arms only to have me pop out again a moment later. He holds nothing back as he adds his jumps and I add mine. He spins me back and forth, and then ducks down to the ground and spins me by tapping my legs so I know to when to change directions. The deejay plays three Cumbia songs in a row, and we dance them all. At the end, I give him a big hug. So far, that was my favorite dance of the night.

"You are such a good dancer!" He tells me.

"Thank you, but only because I had a good partner," I answer.

"You dance both Salsa and Cumbia, right? I see you at the Havana Night Club a lot."

"Yes, I love dancing both."

"I only dance Cumbia. One day, you'll have to teach me Salsa," and with that he walks away back towards the bar.

"Where did you learn to dance Cumbia?" I hear Suzy ask as she appears on my right side.

"At the Havana Night Club. Whenever I get frustrated at how hard it is to learn Salsa, I go over to the other side of the night club where they play Cumbia music. There is a guy there who I've never actually talked to, but I've nicknamed the Cumbia King, because he dances in a way that I can catch on easily," I share my secret with Suzy.

"The Cumbia King? I like it. I might have to search for him one day," she laughs. "By the way, are you and Esteban dating?"

"What makes you think that?" I ask.

"Well, you two dance a lot together. I just wondered, because he was watching you when you were outside talking to your friend. I've never seen him act like that," Suzy looks at me. I can't read her. Is she fishing for gossip or is she simply curious about Esteban?

"We've went on a few dates," I try to say it as nonchalant as possible.

"Who is that other girl he's with?" She asks.

"A student he teaches in Oxnard," I answer.

"Just between us, I think it would benefit him if he danced more with you. I think you could help advertise his classes," as she finishes her sentence we're interrupted by a guy inviting her onto the floor. I have no idea of what to make of what she said.

Before I can think more about it, Mike and Pablo come up to me.

"We're leaving," Pablo says as he gives me a goodbye hug.

"Thank you for everything, Pablo. It was great seeing you again."

"Anything for you, Scarlet," he gives me one last kiss on the cheek.

 Mike takes his turn at giving me a hug.

"We didn't dance again," I tell him. Between worrying about Esteban and learning to dance from Pablo, I realize Mike and I hardly talked this evening.

"I'm not ready yet, but one day," Mike makes me a promise I know he intends to never keep.

"Mike, I want to thank you," I look him in the eye.

"What for?" He asks.

"For bringing Pablo, I know you did it on purpose to help me, and it did. A lot," as I say these words I watch for his reaction to confirm I'm right.

"What gave it away?"

"Nothing could have dragged you back here for another Salsa Night, except to help a friend," I tell him.

"Well, I can't promise that I will make coming here a habit," Mike softens his voice as he says the last few words, "but I hope it helped."

"It did," and with that final sentiment two gorgeous men leave the club.

The men from Santa Barbara keep me busy on the dance floor. It's fun to dance with them in my hometown. Pablo is right. When I dance with someone they become my world. I give them my full attention. This helps distract me from seeing who Esteban is dancing with. I have no desire to watch him dance with Melinda. No good can come from it. Eventually, I get tired and decide to take a break and walk outside.

I'm not alone. Esteban follows me out.

"Are you having a good time?" He asks.

"It's okay," I answer.

"You've been dancing the whole night. I haven't been able to get close to you," he says as he closes the distance between us.

"Well, you said you wanted to dance with Melinda," I answer back.

"For only one song," he takes my hand.

I remember what Angie told me. I have to be honest with him and share how I feel. Seriously, what do I have to lose? I'm not happy with the way things are going.

"Esteban, I want you to teach me how to dance with you, as partners," I lay my cards on the table.

"I told you that you have to practice the basic first, and besides that you live too far away. We wouldn't be able to practice enough. Melinda learns fast because she gets to practice with me almost every day."

"I have Monday off since it's a holiday. I know you're not working either. My boys will be with their father for the day. I want to come to Oxnard, and I want you to practice with me. I want to practice dancing together as partners." After finally getting the words out there, I watch for his reaction.

"That's a long drive just to learn Salsa," he answers. He shakes his head. "You know it doesn't matter to me if you're a good dancer or not. I like you. Dancing is separate from being in a relationship."

Is it? I wonder. For me the dancing and the relationship seems intertwined. If I'm around Esteban, I'm going to want to dance with him.

"It's important to me. I want to learn," I stand my ground.

"Look, last time I tried to teach you it was obvious you didn't practice. I expect all my students to practice or it's a waste of my time."

"Okay, I understand that you think I didn't practice. Maybe that's because it didn't look like it to you, but I'm only going to say this once more, I did," as I say this I feel my cheeks flush with heat. I try to calm myself and continue on, "I want you to teach me, and you are going to have to just trust that I'm practicing even if it doesn't look like it. Maybe I just learn slower than anyone else you've ever met. I'm fine with that. But I mean this, never again tell me I didn't practice."

"I don't know, Scarlet. I'm a strict teacher," Esteban looks away.

I've wanted Esteban to teach me since our first dance together. I remember the first night I watched him dancing and thought he had something special that I could learn. Something that I was chasing to become. The excitement of him offering to give me a dance lesson. The disappointment of hearing about another girl living out my dream day after day. The hurt I feel mounted on top of all the other disappointments I've had since my husband left. At this moment, I'm ready to give up and move on.

"Look, I'm going to learn to dance whether you teach me or not. I wanted it to be you, but if you don't want to teach me that's fine. I'll find someone else," I turn to walk away.

"Wait, okay. Monday. If you're willing to make the drive. We'll practice Monday," he takes my hand and pulls me into him.

"Okay, Monday I'll be there," I can feel a smile break out on my face. "I think I'm going to head home now. My boys will be up early, and I want to take them out somewhere since it's my day off."

"Not without this first," and with those words he kisses me softly, passionately, a hello, goodbye and see you later kiss.

I spoke my mind, said what I wanted, and I didn't fall apart.

Chapter 19 Dancing on the Beach

I love the drive to Oxnard. Just beyond Carpinteria, the highway rests close to the ocean. The blue is unbelievable, and I feel humbled looking at it. For ten years, I lived away from the ocean. I didn't' realize how much I missed it until I returned home to California.

The Salsa music infuses the car. I'm not listening to Esteban's songs. I'm listening to my music. My mind's eye shows me dancing wildly, spinning, doing moves I've never seen before, and I'm not sure are even possible. My partner always changes. I can never quite make out his face, but he loves the way I move. The drive passes quickly with my mind elsewhere, and I find myself parked in front of Esteban's house.

It's a simple white house with a well-taken care of yard lined with succulent plants around the borders. The neighborhood is working class with one-story houses tucked in close to one another. I gather my nerves and walk up to ring the doorbell. It's silly, but he still makes me nervous.

"Hi there, come on in," Esteban gives me a kiss and lets me inside. "How was the drive?"

"It was nice. The sun was shining, and the ocean was beautiful." Like the outside of the house, the inside is both simple and clean. There is no artwork on the walls and no clutter on the floor. The walls are white. The living room has a large sofa and love seat both upholstered in black leather. The room smells clean as though it was mopped this morning. In front of the sofa there is a black coffee table with nothing on it, no candles, magazines or flowers. The décor suggests a hard-working man who takes time to clean, but doesn't spend much time living here.

"I like your place."

"Thanks," Esteban tells me as he picks up his car keys. It looks like he's getting ready to leave.

"Are we going somewhere? I thought we were going to practice."

"We're going somewhere else to practice," he tells me.

"Why?" I ask.

He laughs, "Because if we try to practice here we're going to get interrupted."

"By who?"

"My family," he answers.

"They live here with you?"

"Not in the house, but all around me. My parents live in the house across the street. One brother lives next door. Another brother lives two blocks down. A third brother lives three blocks over in that direction. And one more brother lives two minutes away. They stop by unannounced, and if they see you they won't leave," he smiles. "I haven't brought a girl home to meet my family in about twenty years."

"Why?" I ask.

"I was engaged once back when I was in my early twenties. She broke off the engagement the day before the wedding. I haven't found anyone I've wanted to introduce to my family since."

"I'm sorry. You must have been really hurt."

"Yes, but I was also young. I can't imagine how my life would have turned out if I had married her. It probably would have been a mistake. Still, it took a long time to recover." We head out of the house. "Let's take my car. I think I know a place we can practice."

It's a short car ride to our destination. I find myself in a beach parking lot. Esteban parks us next to a more secluded stretch of sidewalk that is nice and wide, allowing us room to dance. I'm wearing my black flats. They don't have too much traction. I should be able to spin. I wouldn't want to make a habit of practicing out here. I can't imagine it would be good for my joints. However, it's only for one day, and the setting is ideal. Who can feel stressed dancing next to the ocean?

Esteban leaves his car door open so we can hear the Salsa music on the car stereo. Instead of lecturing me on steps, he takes both my hands and we begin to move. There's no talking between us. He keeps spinning me around him, and the spins are fast. Whenever I mess up or miss a hand signal, he stops and does the step again so I can catch it. We go on like this song after song. Esteban doesn't say a word. He just keeps me moving.

"You're heavy on your feet," Esteban finally talks. "I want your weight more on your toes. Also, when I do the cross body lead I want you to glide with it as you bring your feet together. Most people don't do this. That is why Marco and I move faster than the other guys. If you want to keep up with us, you're going to have to start doing it this way." As he says this, he demonstrates the ladies cross body lead the way he wants me to do it. Then he starts up the music and we practice it together for what feels like a hundred times. I can feel that I'm already dripping with sweat.

I'm dancing on some kind of movie set. The blue sky above and the ocean close by with the music coming from the parked car. The classic story of guy teaches girl to dance. People walk by and take a long look, but we don't stop. We keep dancing.

"I want to learn how to do styling," I tell Esteban in between songs. "I've seen the girls at the clubs do all kinds of things with their hands before they spin. Can you teach me some of that too?"

"I've already taught you a lot of styling," Esteban answers.

"What? You have?"

"Yes"

"When?" I am at a complete loss. I think I would have remembered him teaching me how to style before a turn.

"Have you been practicing your arm movements?" He asks.

"Yes," and it's true. As much as I have come to dislike it I have been faithfully practicing those dreaded sequence of arm movements almost every day. The mind numbing ritual of doing them without stopping one after another for an entire song.

"Good. Do them while your dancing."

"How?"

"Just try it," he says as he takes my hands and gets me moving.

"Do the scoop with the arm up here," he tells me before I spin. I do it and my arm reacts before I have time to think. It flies up without effort, because it has done so a million times already.

"Yes, like that. Now try it here but reach outward instead of up," he says as he takes me for a double spin during a cross body lead. I scoop and stretch outward as I rotate each time. We dance a whole song as I experiment putting in the arm movements in various places. My arms move easily, and because I don't have to think about the motion I play with timing it to the music.

"I can't believe it," I tell him when we stop.

"See, you have styling, and it looks different than the other girls. Most of them just do the same things. This gives you variety. You also have speed and your arms are nice and loose. Most of the ladies styling looks stiff, but this is more natural because of the way you practice," as Esteban finishes his words I see him smile. Something rare in our Salsa lessons.

We dance for what feels like hours. I try different things with my arms by combining the movements, adding my own variations, and seeing where I can add the styling without accidentally hitting him (which has happened a few times already). I'm glad I wore a light tank top and shorts, because I feel the sweat soaking my clothes. Esteban only shows the slightest of perspiration, but then again, he isn't spinning in all directions while twirling his arms around in the air.

Esteban takes me into a double spin and brings me to a sudden stop in his arms. My head still whirling from the spin, he draws me in close for a hug.

"Okay, have you learned enough for one day?" He asks.

"Yes," I answer.

"Are you happy?" He teases.

"Yes, I'm happy." I give him a kiss.

"Let's get something to eat," he puts his arm around me as we walk back to the car.

We pick up some hamburgers and fries at a drive thru and head to the Oxnard harbor. The water is a deep blue that looks so rich in color it seems out of place. Ships line the harbor with silly names painted on their sides. A sea gull walks up and down the pier like a little admiral inspecting the yard. Esteban leads me to a stone bench where we can eat our food and breathe in the marine life surrounding us.

"I want to show you something," he says as he takes out his cell phone. "This is a video of me when I first started taking classes with Luis. I was terrible," he laughs. He holds the phone so we can both watch. "See, there's Luis dancing in front. Do you see that girl next to him? She later went on to win a World Championship too."

I watch the pair leading the class. Luis is tall and lean. Like Esteban, his hair is dark and so are his eyes. He is wearing a red shirt and jeans with black and white dance shoes. His steps are disciplined, but his body moves like water as the music courses through him moving his shoulders, arms, hips and even his head at its every whim. He is a spell-caster, and it's hard to look away. The girl has long red hair and is wearing a black shirt with jeans and red heels. Her footwork is good, but she lacks the finesse of her teacher.

The camera man starts to scan the students dancing. I spot Esteban. He is in the second row. I can barely recognize him. His movements are choppy and out of sync with Luis. You can tell by the serious look on his face that he's trying, but obviously, he's not having much success.

"Oh, wow, that's you," I point out.

"Yeah, I used to dance really bad," he chuckles.

"How did you get better?" I ask.

"Practice, a lot of practice."

"Did you learn most of your combinations from Luis?"

"No, most of my combinations I created myself," he smiles.

"I thought so," I answer back. His creativity is part of what draws me to him. He puts his arm around me, and I rest my head on his shoulders. I take in everything from the vibrant color of the harbor to the sun heating my skin, the scent of his cologne, and the comfort I feel being held by him. I feel at peace, and I haven't felt that for such a long time.

Chapter 20 A Place of My Own

"What are you doing?" Esteban asks when I pick up the phone.

"I'm sitting on my bed talking to you in my new apartment," I answer.

"How did the move go?"

"It was fairly easy since I didn't take much with me."

When the divorce happened, I let my husband have first pick of our things. I sold the majority of what was left. I did, however, keep all of my children's possessions, family scrapbooks, and Christmas and Halloween decorations, which were to me, priceless. By an odd turn of luck, my ex-husband left behind those items I loved the most. My French coffee table and hutch, Classical guitar, and one thrift store picture of a man and woman dancing. This picture seems destined to be mine.

I remember visiting a thrift store one afternoon and being drawn to this picture. I don't know if it was the romantic dance pose or the vibrant color of her blue dress mixed with the black of his tux. It could have been the expression on her face which looked confident and relaxed. The man's face was missing giving the woman center stage. At the time, it seemed silly to spend money on a picture so I left the store without it. A week later, my husband bought it. I never mentioned the picture to him, but somehow he ended up bringing it home. I must admit I was hoping the picture would find its way to me a second time. It's funny what you come to value after twenty years of buying stuff.

I've been working on this move for a couple of weeks now. I love that my parents took us in, but it's time to move on to the next step. My parents still watch my youngest after school and help with dinner on my late nights at work. They've also kept the boys' room intact, so they can sleepover whenever I want a night to myself.

"How does it feel having your own place?" Esteban asks.

"Quiet, but I like it," I answer. My boys and I are quiet people. We read and talk to each other, but we hardly ever watch TV. My ex-husband was the one who always had the TV on, and my parents watch the news twenty-four seven. The house is quieter when there is no background noise.

"Thanksgiving is coming up next week. I have four days off in a row," Esteban shares. "Are you celebrating the holiday at your new apartment or at your mom's house?"

"Well, neither actually. My ex-husband moved to LA about three weeks ago. He wants the boys to visit him. I'm meeting him halfway in Oxnard on Thanksgiving day around noon to drop off the boys. It's sad. I've never spent a holiday without my sons. My parents are in Hawaii visiting my grandparents. So, I guess I'll spend most of the day just driving."

"Do you want to come over after you drop off your boys?" Esteban offers.

"I'd love to, but don't you have plans with your family?"

"Not until the evening. I'm free during the day."

"Yeah, I'd like that. I'll head over to your place after my boys go with their dad."

I talk with Esteban about our day, the way we do every night before bedtime. It's almost like having him here with me. After our call, I feel a little bit better. I've been dreading Thanksgiving ever since I knew I'd be spending most of it alone.

It brings back memories of my teenage years that I would prefer remained buried forever. My father left my mother when I was fourteen. I'm an only child, so I had no siblings to soften the blow. When my mother would work I would be left alone in the house. Unfortunately, since she was a nurse this meant spending most holidays by myself. My father was too busy with his new fiancé to think of visiting his daughter. Once I married and had children of my own, I thought those days of being alone for the holidays were long behind me. I guess I was wrong.

I crawl into bed and pull the covers close. Maybe my whole world has fallen apart, but I'm still here. I have my boys. You could have offered me the sexiest man in Hollywood, billions of dollars, and the career of my dreams, and if it meant leaving my family I wouldn't have taken it. I know what I have, and it is beyond all the riches my mind can imagine. My husband made his choice, and I have made mine. I have what matters most.

Chapter 21 Happy Thanksgiving

"I love you. I'll call you later tonight. Have a good time," I try to hide my sadness as I hug my boys. It's hard letting them go, but I'm not going to cry. I'm not going to do that to them. I will hold it together.

And just like that, they are gone. Packed into the car with their father and off driving away from me on Thanksgiving day. I leave, but I know I won't drive far. I find a parking lot close by and settle there. I fiddle with my makeup and hair. It's better than crying. As I look into the car mirror, I remember the morning hours spent with my boys.

Ben is my early riser. I started my day before him, cooking biscuits and gravy in our tiny kitchen. My goal was to have it done before he woke up, because like me, he wakes up hungry. He's not one to be excited about food, but one thing he looks forward to every holiday is his biscuits and gravy. To him, whatever comes after, turkey, ham, stuffing, potatoes, our traditional lumpia, all of it is anti-climactic. Holidays are all about the biscuits and gravy for breakfast. I never disappoint him.

So, if I had to handpick one part of the day to spend with my boys, this would be it. Just so I could still give this to him. Something normal that he can carry throughout the day. I've promised to teach my youngest how to make biscuits and gravy, so his big brother never forgets to visit him.

After a few deep breaths, I bring myself back to reality and head over to Esteban's place. I am so grateful that I don't have to be alone, even if it's only for a few hours. I'm not sure how I'll get through the evening, but at least, I have this afternoon with Esteban.

"Hello," Esteban tells me as he greets me with a kiss at the door.

"Hi, how's your day going?" I ask.

"Good," he replies as he grabs his car keys sitting on the kitchen table.

"Are we heading out?"

"Yes, I hate to stay inside on my days off. I thought I'd take us to the harbor in Ventura."

"That sounds perfect." We could be going anywhere. I just don't want to be alone.

We hop in his car and drive for about twenty minutes and find ourselves at the harbor. It has a different feel from the Oxnard Harbor. This one is a little more touristy. It has fancy shops lining one side of the sidewalk while the other side shows the vast harbor with its docked boats. There are mosaics of turtles, seamen, and other aspects of marine life accenting various walls. I imagine it must be busy on the weekends, but today it is quiet.

Esteban takes my arm in his as we stroll along. I can feel the warmth from the sun overhead, but it's comfortable rather than overwhelming.

"Have you settled into your apartment?" Esteban asks.

"Almost, I have the basics set up, but I don't have any pictures on the walls yet."

"Do you like the place?"

"I like that the apartment complex is nice and quiet, and the boys and I feel safe there."

I can't bring myself to tell him the whole truth. I don't have it in me to decorate my new apartment. I just can't seem to do it. My house had personal touches with painted walls, pictures of my boys, and souvenirs from all the places we had lived. My new apartment has everything I need to survive, but I can't seem to get myself to do anything more with it.

We walk along the small pier and peer down at the rocks that border the water's edge. I try to look for crabs, and at first see nothing. But once my eye catches one, I notice them all crawling about the rocks. It gives me the shivers. Esteban and I have fun pointing out each crab.

The hours pass by as we talk, grab coffee, and stroll about. Before long, the sun starts to make its way down, and I know it won't be long before I head home.

"Do you want me to come to Lompoc with you?" Esteban asks as we make our way back to his car.

"Isn't your family expecting you?"

"Yes, but I have a big family. I've spent every Thanksgiving with them. I think they'll be okay without me for one time."

He takes my hand and spins me into his arms. I laugh. How can I say no?

"I don't have much food in the apartment. I wasn't planning on cooking anything special. The boys are away with their father for the next few days so I figured I was only cooking for one." I imagine his family will have loads of food. It seems unfair to ask him to follow me back to Lompoc only to eat whatever I can whip together at the last minute.

"No big deal. I know a place we can have dinner before heading out. If you want, we could come back here tomorrow for dancing. The 805 is having a Salsa Night. When do your boys come home?"

"I pick them up here in Oxnard Saturday afternoon," I tell him.

"That would work out perfectly. What do you think?"

"Yes, I think it's a plan," I can feel myself smiling. I feel relieved. I don't have to face the empty apartment alone. I'm also excited at the prospect of an unexpected Salsa Night. Not to mention, I get to spend the next couple of days with Esteban.

Chapter 22 Just the Two of Us

Esteban takes us to a restaurant with a name I can't pronounce. Since my return to California, I've encountered a lot of people who speak Spanish and many are surprised that I don't. During my childhood, I didn't hear much Spanish in my little town of Lompoc, so I never learned. I love the language. It fills the music I dance to every day. I'm trying my best to learn to speak it, but like dancing, it might take a while.

I find the bright colors of the restaurant inviting. It has a melody of yellows and oranges that play nicely with the blue tables and chairs. Who could feel sad here? Along one wall, there extends a large mural of a fiesta scene. It looks as though it is a throwback to the 1950s and centers around a long wooden table with people sharing a meal. They're clothed in vibrant colors with the women wearing flowered dresses and a few of the men donning Sombreros. All have happy faces and most are captured forever laughing. As I look closer, my eye catches one that looks vaguely familiar. Is it? No, it couldn't be.

"Esteban, is that Elvis?" I ask as I point to one of the painted men playing guitar, singing, with black shiny hair and a signature smile that only exists on one other face that I know.

"You know what? I think it is," he laughs. "I never noticed that before."

"And that one," I point to another man sitting at the painted fiesta table, "he has to be James Dean. Who else has those eyes? All he's missing is a cigarette hanging from his mouth." This is fun. Once you recognize one familiar face, the others begin to pop out. At first they're hidden because you're not expecting them to be there, but once you look closer you can't help but notice the distinctive features of each famous person.

"That girl has to be a young Elizabeth Taylor," I point out.

"The man with his arm wrapped around her is Pedro Infante," Esteban smiles as he recognizes the face.

"Who is he?" I ask.

"He's a famous Mexican actor. I grew up watching his films with my mom." As Esteban finishes telling me this, the waitress comes and takes our order. I let Esteban order for the both of us, since I want to try something new.

When the food comes it looks rather simple and ordinary. Esteban and I are each given a plate with rice, beans, and chicken. The waitress also brings corn tortillas and salsa for Esteban and I to share. I grab my fork and am ready to dig in when Esteban stops me.

"Try it this way," he says as he takes one of the tortillas tears off a portion and then uses it to gather a chunk of chicken, beans and rice which he tops off with some salsa before taking a bite. I give it a try. It tastes amazing. I also realize that I am hungrier than I thought. I am devouring my dinner quite quickly. Have I eaten since the biscuits and gravy this morning? I can't remember. Whether it is the mix of the flavors combined in the tortilla or my intense hunger, this dinner is perfect for Thanksgiving.

"Thanks, Esteban. This tastes so good," I manage to say in between mouthfuls.

"I'm glad you like it," Esteban answers as he tears off another tortilla.

After satisfying our appetites, we make the drive back to Lompoc. It's dark. I'm guessing it's about seven o'clock. The roadways are somewhat empty. Salsa music fuels the car as we discuss little things to pass the time.

Esteban asks me to stop at a Mexican grocery store when we enter Lompoc. I didn't even know we had one, but Esteban remembered seeing it. I'm surprised they are open so late on Thanksgiving. I follow Esteban as he gathers Mexican pastries, tortillas, eggs, tomatoes, onions, peppers, jalapenos, onions, and even buys some kind of flat frying pan meant to heat the tortillas. He took a wild guess that I didn't have one. He's right, of course. After stocking up on the supplies, we head over to my apartment.

I invite Esteban into my new place. We settle in as I put away the groceries.

"I like your place," Esteban tells me.

"Thanks. It has a nice feel to it. I haven't decorated yet, but it feels cozy. The neighbors are friendly. Everyone keeps to themselves but if you see them in the walkways they are nice enough to say hello and smile." That is one thing I really like about my apartment complex. Neighbors who are kind but not busybodies. "Make yourself at home. If you want you can change into something more comfortable, and there are extra towels if you want to take a shower. Do you like tea?"

"Yeah, I'd love some tea, and I think I'll take you up on that shower, if that's all right."

"Of course," I give Esteban a kiss on the cheek and grab a couple of towels for him.

While he showers, I call my boys. It's good to hear their voices. I want them to know that I'm thinking about them. I'm careful to keep my voice from showing any signs of sadness. They need to believe that their mom is okay so they don't worry. I also keep the conversation short, so it doesn't take time away from what they're doing with their dad.

By the time Esteban finishes his shower, our tea is ready.

"Can I use your computer?" Esteban asks.

"Sure," I answer as I take my first sip of tea.

"I want to show you something," he tells me as he motions me to sit next to him on the couch.

"This is a video of Luis dancing with one of his best partners."

In one glance, you can tell that they are professionals. The woman combines Salsa with ballet. She is extremely flexible, and Luis floats her in the air as though she is weightless. Her spins are fast and numerous. She spins low to the ground, high in the air, looking down, looking up, and while performing different body contortions. And although I enjoy watching them dance, I have one thought that keeps gnawing at me. There is no way I can ever dance like that. I'm not flexible. Even when I was five years old I couldn't bend down and touch my toes, not even when I took ballet as a teenager no matter how much I stretched and tried. My body was not made to do that. I can see by the look on Esteban's face that this is what he wants.

"They are beautiful together," I tell him,

"You have the ability to spin fast like her."

"Really? Do you think so?"

"Yes, if you practice you can do it."

"Maybe." It feels good to have him give me a compliment. It's possible I could learn to spin fast. I could see with a lot of practice that would be within the realm of possibility. But the rest of it, the aerial spins, splits, dips and high kicks will never happen. It's not in my DNA. For myself, it doesn't bother me one bit. I just love to dance. But Esteban? I think he wants something more.

While I'm thinking this, Esteban changes the computer to something else. It looks like a black and white movie.

"Remember the picture of Pedro Infante we saw at the restaurant?" Esteban asks.

136

"Yeah," I answer.

"This is one of his movies. My mom and I used to watch his movies all the time," as he says this he relaxes on the couch and puts his arm around me drawing me close to him. After watching for a few minutes, he starts to move towards the computer again.

"I can change it. I know you don't understand much Spanish. What would you like to watch?" He asks.

"This is perfect. If you don't mind translating for me?" I ask.

"Really? You'd like to watch this?"

"Yes," I tell him, and I can see by the look on his face he's happy. I relax into his arms.

I feel like love at first sight. I almost don't want to tell Esteban that my mother and I used to watch old movies too. She worked long hours so she was always tired and often sleeping, but when an old movie came on she would take the time to watch it with me. The plot lines were always something silly and frivolous. It felt like being transported to a different time with stylish clothes, old fashion backdrops and out-of-date customs. I haven't watched a classic for decades. This reminds me how much I loved it as a kid.

The language barrier is problematic, but that doesn't take away from my enjoyment. I understand a few words here and there, and Esteban translates the rest as needed. As in most classic movies, the acting is overdone so it's easy to figure out the basic storyline. This movie is very similar to the ones I used to watch, with lots of singing and dancing. However, the settings and costumes are new to me, and therefore have an exotic touch. The classics I grew up with had the familiar boy meets girl story, which usually took place in a social vacuum where no harsh realities existed. This plot has more depth, taking on issues such as poverty and discrimination. This fascinates me. I snuggle up to Esteban on the couch, and do nothing else but take him and the movie in.

"Thanks for sharing this with me. It reminds me of the movies I used to watch with my mom when I was little," I tell Esteban as the movie ends.

"I'm glad you liked it," he answers as we linger with my head resting on his shoulder and his arms still wrapped around me.

"I'm tired. Are you ready to go to bed?" I ask.

"Yes," Esteban answers as he pulls me closer for a kiss.

Chapter 23 Dancing with El Grupo

Esteban and I are lazy getting up. I'm usually awake by the early morning hours, but today I take my time. When we finally do start our day, we are hungry.

"I'll make us breakfast," I tell him as I head towards the kitchen.

"Let me make breakfast. I bought some things to cook for you," Esteban shares as he passes me in the hallway and kisses my cheek.

Nothing is sexier than seeing Esteban enter the kitchen with the intent to cook for me. I put on some Cumbia music. Good music helps to make good food.

I help chop up the onions, tomatoes, and jalapenos. He fries them up in some olive oil and then adds the eggs. He throws in a little salt and pepper. I make the tea. He warms up the tortillas on my new frying pan. It's a simple and quick to cook breakfast, the kind I like.

We sit down at my kitchen table. We tear the tortillas and use the little pieces to pick up the egg scramble, and top It off with some salsa. It's delicious.

"What do you want to do today?" I ask.

"We can hang around Lompoc for a while, but we should head back to Oxnard by the afternoon. I have a Salsa practice today with the group. Do you want to come?"

"Of course."

"We'll need to pick up a cake from the bakery. We practice at Fernando's house, and he's cooking dinner for all of us." As he tells me this, I get more excited. I finally get to hang out with everyone.

I have daydreamed about practicing with his dance group countless times. It's hard to believe that today I will actually be there.

We take our time packing up for Oxnard. I take three dresses with me for dancing. I can't seem to make up my mind which one looks better on me. We grab some lunch and head on down the highway.

Around three in the afternoon, I find myself at Fernando's house. He lives across town from Esteban's place. It's a small house. The outside is painted a light brown color. Succulents and cacti border the fenced yard. There is nothing extravagant or eye-catching about the house, but the place looks well-kept. We ring the doorbell, and Fernando welcomes us in.

He is taller than the both of us. He has a large build which isn't fat, but is also far away from skinny. He reminds me of the Jolly Green Giant minus the green. His smile is in the shape of a wide grin. He offers his hand to shake mine and welcomes me into his home.

His house has a homey feel with knick-knacks and pictures hung on the walls. Comfy is the best word to describe it. In the center of the room, there is a well-worn couch with throw blankets draped over the sides and an apple cinnamon candle burning on the coffee table.

We're the last to arrive. I see Marco sitting at the kitchen table next to a girl with long brown hair pulled up on top of her head in a messy bun. Melinda won't be joining us until later tonight at the 805. So, we're all here.

"Marisol, this is Scarlet," Fernando handles the introduction.

"Hi Scarlet," Marisol says as she gets up to give me a hug.

"Hi, it's nice to meet you," I answer. "Have you been dancing with these guys for long?"

"I've been coming off and on for a couple of months," she tells me as she sits back down at the table. "How long have you been dancing?"

"Not very long. I'm still pretty new at it." I take a seat next to her. She has a nice smile and seems friendly. I listen as Esteban starts talking to Marco about people they know at the clubs. After a short while, they start to head outside and Marisol and I follow along.

The backyard looks double the size I would expect given the small house. We walk out to a large patio area that will serve as our dance floor. Beyond the patio, there is a generous green yard, perhaps half an acre, bordered by a plain wooden fence. Esteban starts up the music.

The music changes the landscape. It permeates the patio inviting us to dance, and that's what we do. Marco and Esteban stand in the front and start with the basic. I guess this is the warm up for every practice. Marisol and I find spots behind them, and Fernando joins in with us.

The Salsa basic is not so tedious when done in a group. I look around at the other dancers. Esteban and Marco are perfectly in sync, arms and feet moving at the same time effortlessly. Fernando is on time as well, but it looks slightly different on him. I can't figure out if its due to his larger body type or if he's just less graceful. Marisol almost has the timing down, but she does play the hide and seek game of losing it and finding it. I notice that she points her toes straight ahead instead of outward like Cindy taught me and that her movements are choppy as if she is still trying to drill it into muscle memory.

The warm up continues on with Esteban leading us through a variety of steps. He calls each step out a moment before we're expected to execute it. All of us are trying to keep up with him. I don't feel so discouraged now that I see the others are having a tougher time than me, even Marco struggles reading Esteban's mind.

"Okay, let's start with the combinations. We'll practice the first ten." Esteban stops the music and directs us to dance together. He motions to Marco to dance with me. Fernando dances with Marisol.

Esteban starts the music. To my surprise, the guys know what to do. They take Marisol and I through the first ten combinations over and over again until the music stops.

Marco is easy to follow. There are lots of spins, so I concentrate on spotting to prevent dizziness. In some ways, he is easier to read than Esteban. He gives more clues. Marco exaggerates his arm motions to signal me to cross in front of him. If I give a confused look, he'll give a nod of the head or dart his eyes in the direction he wants me to spin. His timing is fluid with the music, infused with grace, nothing abrasive or out of sync. I feel relaxed. He doesn't make me nervous like Esteban.

"Marco, do the next ten combinations," Esteban instructs us.

Marco leads me through the combinations counting them off out loud beginning with number eleven. There is no hesitation in Marco's movements. His body has memorized every twist and turn in the proper sequence. I can follow along because Marco's lead is crystal clear. When we finish, Esteban gives me a few pointers. Esteban takes both of my hands and guides me into a double spin while I travel across him to the other side.

"Try it again, but step out more so you can cover more ground while you spin." He leads me into the double spins again, but this time a little slower so I have time to do the move correctly. He's right. His advice makes it easier to complete the revolutions and end facing him.

Esteban has Fernando try the same combinations with Marisol. They run into trouble at the midway mark. Fernando has forgotten the moves. Esteban takes time to teach them while Marco and I practice all twenty combinations non-stop.

It feels incredible. This is what I've always wanted. Dancing with friends, learning the secrets of how to move with a partner, and bringing something out of myself that has been waiting to awaken. I'm still not sure what it is exactly, but I feel closer to it. My mind is too preoccupied trying to read Marco's hand signals to think of anything else. A place where there is only the moment. No divorce, no sadness, no ex-husband, regrets or blame. Life is simple. It is a dance.

The practice goes on for a couple of hours. We never make it past the twenty combinations. I don't remember a single one, but I'm learning how to follow. Afterwards, Fernando feeds us. I listen as they talk about their nights out at the clubs and the other dancers they encounter. They share their good dances and bad ones. It reminds me of my own experiences. I'm with people who understand me. I sit back and listen as I wonder what lies ahead at the 805.

Chapter 24 The 805

Esteban opens my car door. He looks handsome dressed in black. Tonight, I'm wearing a black and white dress with silver heels. I take his hand, and together we walk into the club.

The 805 is more casual than the Havana Night Club, but a little more upscale than La Pura Vida. As we enter, I see a restaurant-style seating area with booths lining the walkway to the dance floor. Along the wall to the left there is a long bar that stretches half the length of the club. People are busy eating and drinking with friends. The place is packed. Tucked in the back of the club is a dancing area about half the size of the one at La Pura Vida. The deejay plays music from a stage to the right.

"Hey, Esteban," a guy gives Esteban a quick hug while holding a beer in his free hand. He steps to the side and looks at me waiting to be introduced.

"This is Scarlet. Scarlet, this here is Pedro." I shake his hand and say hello.

This scenario repeats with a dozen different people as we make our way to a table next to the dance floor.

"I think you must know everyone here," I tell Esteban.

"Almost, I've seen them every week for the past year."

My eyes catch Fernando dancing with Marisol. Her hair is worn half up/half down with loose curls touching her shoulders. She spins around Fernando in a peach-colored dress. The Jolly Green Giant shines a grin down at her as she travels across him to the other side.

Next to them, I see Marco and Melinda moving faster with more complicated combinations. All is going well until Marco lets her loose to solo. He seamlessly switches to dancing on his own with intricate foot patterns. Melinda looks lost and sticks strictly to the basic until he returns.

I recognize one couple from La Pura Vida. The man with the Fedora hat and the woman with silver heels. Of course, tonight they are wearing different outfits, but their dancing style remains the same. Choreographed. Oh, and the man is still sporting the Fedora. I spot another couple that looks like they are instructors as well. In fact, it looks like they are competing with the Fedora couple for the crowd's attention. The man appears to be in his mid-forties while the girl looks like she's in her early twenties. He spins her fast and furious, and she tosses her long hair around every chance she gets. Both lady dancers are throwing in body rolls and styling with their arm movements as much as possible. To me, it's overdone and unnatural, but the crowd seems to like it. The men add the show-stopping dips and flips, each trying to steal the audience's attention. I have to admit its eye-catching, but it just isn't for me.

"Who are they?" I point the couples out to Esteban. He starts with the first couple that I remember from La Pura Vida.

"That's Jose and Stella. They teach at a dance studio in Santa Barbara. Jose has been dancing for over twenty years, and I think Stella has been around for the past five. They're well known in the area." Esteban's voice is matter of fact in its tone, but I sense something else in his body language. I don't think he likes them.

"And the other couple?" I ask.

"Martin and Margarita. They're also instructors. They teach in Camarillo. Martin has been dancing for as long as Jose, but Margarita has only been dancing for less than a year. She's Martin's latest girlfriend." Again, Esteban's voice is calm, but the look on his face tells me something isn't right.

"There you guys are," Fernando's voice rings out as he comes to give us hugs. I see Marisol standing next to him so I walk over and give her a hello hug as well.

Next, Marco and Melinda join us.

"Hi, Marco," I greet him as I walk over to complete the round of hugs.

I decide to make the first move and approach Melinda, "You must be Melinda. I'm Scarlet. I saw you in Lompoc, but didn't get a chance to say hello," I offer her a hug too. I love being part of this group. I want to try my best to get along with everyone.

"It's nice to see you again," Melinda answers. She doesn't say much after that, but at least she hugs me back.

I hear one of my favorite songs playing. Marco asks me to dance. He is the perfect partner. Marco is so smooth that I feel myself floating with him. His combinations are always changing, but there is a continuous flow. I tune the rest of the world out-my worries, anxieties, sadness-so that I can follow him and feel the music the way he does.

I'm surrounded by people on all sides. I feel their energy, and I love it. A weird thought creeps into my head that often surfaces when I dance. What if this is my last chance to dance ever? Who can predict the twists and turns of life? Whoever I'm with, whether he be the best dancer or worst, if he smells good or bad, shouldn't I make the most of it?

I catch a glimpse of Esteban and Melinda dancing to my right. Marco smiles and nods at them. Both Esteban and Marco have non-stop combinations. It takes my full attention to read the signals fast enough. Then I feel it. Marco lets me go to style on my own.

I love the freedom. I try to give no thought as to what my moves should be. Instead, I clear my mind and let my body react to the music. I practice Esteban's steps every day, so I have raw material to work with. The magic comes in letting go and seeing what comes in the moment. I make my mind a blank slate in hopes of creating something new. It works. I can feel my body moving in ways I haven't before, and will never remember again.

Marco comes back to me and the dance continues on. Every guy interprets the music his own way. His own dance fingerprint. As a follower, I get to experience the music a myriad of ways in a single night. It's as if I'm invited into a private world which includes only the two of us.

The dance ends, and Esteban finds me for the next one. This is a wild ride. He can do more with me now, because I've been practicing his combinations. He's an incredibly fast dancer. It's hard to read the signals quick enough to stay on beat. Dancing with Esteban almost requires precognition to finish the spins on time.

I see Jose and Stella dancing beside us to my right. As fast as Jose is he can't keep up with Esteban. I can't catch a long look, but when I do glance over I see there is no contest. We're flying, and I'm hanging on for dear life. I love it.

Esteban lets me go, and then something unexpected happens. I freeze. I don't freeze entirely. I'm still dancing, turning, and coming up with something to do while he freestyles, but all of my creativity is blocked. I'm a shadow of myself. I've disconnected with the music and whatever magic I normally feel is gone.

Esteban brings me back to him and we continue on. I can feel he's disappointed. He doesn't say anything, but in the connection between us I can feel it. That doesn't slow the combinations down. I keep twirling about until the song ends. He gives me a gentle kiss on the cheek.

"Scarlet, I think we should dance with other people tonight. It will help both of us to grow as dancers," he tells me.

I'm a little surprised. I wasn't expecting this. I can't help but wonder if it has to do with my freezing when we danced on our own. Is it really that important to him to show off? Everything was going so perfectly. Spending time together, practicing with new friends, and living my fantasy of dancing with Esteban until the wee hours of the morning. I don't understand. Why? This isn't what I wanted. I don't know what to say. I don't think I said anything, but maybe I did, because he heads over to Stella and asks her to dance.

The two of them dancing together attracts attention. The promoter grabs his phone and starts recording. Stella adds styling to the combinations. She's almost fast enough to keep up with Esteban, but not quite. I can tell Esteban slows the combinations down to accommodate Stella's arm movements and head rolls, and also to disguise her inability to follow his signals quick enough. I doubt anyone in the crowd would notice since they don't know what he is capable of at full speed. I quit watching after a few minutes. It's too depressing.

My night then becomes like every other Salsa Night. Song after song, I dance with different men. I keep wondering if Esteban is going to make his way back to me, but he doesn't. Luckily, I'm lost in the music while I'm dancing and temporarily forget about Esteban. Unfortunately, I remember my predicament at the end of every song. This isn't what I wanted. Tonight, I wanted to be with him.

An hour flies by on the dance floor before I take a break and walk outside. There's a patio area in the back. It has a couple of tall heaters to take the bite off the night chill. I sit at a bench and watch people come and go. I don't recognize anyone. Everyone from Esteban's dance group is out on the floor. Throughout the evening, I've seen a few people I know from Santa Barbara, but none are out on the patio.

Only outside in the fresh air do my emotions catch up with me. Away from the dancing, it hits me how sad and lonely I feel. I'm always toughing things out on my own. Most of the time, I am too busy dancing to acknowledge it, but right now I have nothing to distract me. I thought tonight would be different, but it's not.

"Can I join you?" A man's voice takes me away from my thoughts.

"Sure," I answer. It's the man with the Fedora hat. He's more handsome up close. He looks to be about my age, and in great shape from the dancing. Dark hair, dark eyes, and dark skin that remind me of Esteban.

"I'm Jose," he offers me his hand.

"Scarlet, nice to meet you."

"Are you taking a break?" He asks.

"Yes, just catching my second wind before I go in for more." He seems nice in person, not as flashy as he appears on the dance floor.

"Is this your first time here? I haven't seen you before."

"Yes, I've been to La Pura Vida, but this is my first time at the 805. I live in Lompoc."

"Lompoc? That's a long drive. You didn't come by yourself, did you?" He smiles.

"No," I laugh. The music changes to a new song, and I can see it change the expression on his face. I recognize the song. It's a good one, the type that calls to you.

"Are you ready to dance?" He asks as he offers his hand.

"Yes," I say as I slip my hand into his.

We head out to the dance floor. He places us next to Esteban and Melinda. I see Jose send a signal to the promoter to record us. My eyes catch Esteban and I can see the competitiveness rise in his face. This isn't about me. He wants to out dance Jose. And right

149

now, I want to out dance Esteban. I clear my mind, and let the music move through me. I connect with it letting it touch every part of my body. I focus on my partner and remember that, like always, if this was my last dance ever, I would want to enjoy it.

Jose is a skilled instructor. Even though I've never danced with him before I can read his signals easily. He's not moving as fast as Esteban, so that helps. I can see in his eyes that he is surprised at my speed and how quickly I react. I feel him experimenting with me seeing how far he can push the limits and still lead me. I feel comfortable with him, like I can do nothing wrong. He can fix any mistake.

Out of the corner of my vision, I catch glimpses of Esteban and Melinda. I feel sorry for her. Fueled by his competitiveness, Esteban is giving it all he has, and Melinda is barely hanging on. I'm surprised she can breathe. It takes a lot of cardio to keep up with him. She looks miserable.

My partner has a grin on his face which makes me smile in return. With me, his moves are not choreographed. Whatever we're creating, we're creating together. The moment I miss a cue he just smiles and gets me back on course, as if nothing really matters. This brings out the best in me.

Jose spins me into him and pushes me back out. I play with the arm movements Esteban taught me, lifting my hand overhead and letting it spiral down as Jose pulls me into him again. We touch hands gently as he leans me into his body. Once more, he pushes me away, but this time when he brings me in he leans my body further into him and drags me across the floor. At the end, he drops me low to one side and quickly brings me up to face him. My hair follows, being tossed upward by the momentum and falling to my shoulders for the finish. This is new to me, and I love it. He takes me through a dozen combinations which have me spinning, him spinning and other twists about each other which I know I will never remember. I simply look for his hands and feel for what they want me to do. Then he sets me loose to dance on my own.

I feel the magic. All of the surprises have loosened my body and placed me in the comic realm where nothing can be taken seriously and therefore anything is doable. I could care less what happens and that's when I can feel myself give into the dance. My head stops its incessant chatter. There is nothing left but the music coursing through me. Practicing every day gives my body more than enough moves to work with as I let go of my grip on trying to do things correctly, and just let the dance be whatever it wants. I'm happy, and by the look on Jose's face, he's happy too.

He takes his time gathering me to him again. We end the dance in a flurry of twirls and a dip which lasts for only a second before he brings up in his arms. I give him a quick hug to show my gratitude, and he holds me close for a moment and kisses my cheek.

"That was beautiful. You're amazing. Thank you," he tells me before letting me go. His words feel sincere so I can't help but smile.

"Thank you. That was great," I say to him before walking away. I head outside again to recover and collect myself.

I sit at the same bench by the tall heater, but this time I feel rejuvenated. The stars look brighter and the moon is brilliant. I feel like a kid staring out a car window late at night in wonder.

Esteban sits beside me.

"Hi there," I nudge him gently.

"Are you having fun, Scarlet?" He asks.

"Yes, are you?" I answer.

"Yes," he puts his arm around me. "Do you want something to drink?" Now that he mentions it, I am thirsty. I don't think I'll make it through the night without water.

"Sure, my usual water," I laugh. I doubt there are any other Salseras here that consume only water. I'm an oddity. "Do you want me to come with you?"

"No, you can relax here. Save my seat, okay?" He gives me a kiss before walking away. It is then that I notice Jose standing by the open door to the patio. By the time I get a good look, he's heading back towards the dance floor.

I walk over to the doorway. I watch Jose as he asks Melinda to dance. She agrees. I lean against the back wall. I want to watch them dance. Jose is smiling like he did with me. He starts with simple combinations which Melinda seems to follow. As the dance continues on, I see Jose trying out more complicated patterns, but Melinda isn't sure what to do. Jose helps her along and gets them back on beat when she throws them off. I can tell he has to hold back with her, but like a gentleman he doesn't show any frustration. He keeps smiling. I doubt Melinda even realizes what he's doing. Jose lets her go after a spin so they can freestyle. He does his fancy footwork while keeping an eye on Melinda. She doesn't do a lot. Some Salsa basics, side to side steps, and some Suzy Q's, there is no flavor or improvisation. Jose comes back to her quickly and they continue on.

Pablo was right. I can see for myself what he saw. I've listened to Esteban sing her praises night after night. How many times did he tell me she was a natural dancer? She had such passion for dancing! No, that is not what I see. I wonder why Esteban cannot see how much I love to dance and how hard I work at it every day. Why is he blind to both of us?

"There you are," I hear Esteban's voice as he comes up beside me with my drink.

"Thank you," I kiss his cheek. He stands next to me as we watch the dancers.

"The good dancers are in LA," he shares with me.

"The dancers here seem pretty good."

"No, they are nothing compared to the dancers you find in LA," Esteban says as he continues to stare at the crowd dancing.

"Will you take me to LA?" I ask.

"One day, when you're ready."

"I'm ready now," I answer.

"Almost, but if you wait and get a little better, you'll enjoy it more. One day, I'll take you," he smiles back at me. "Are you ready to dance again?" He extends his hand. We put our drinks down and return to dancing.

Instead of walking me onto the floor, Esteban winds me up and sets me loose to spin to the middle of the floor. He then rushes in towards me and takes me into a cross body lead which leads to endless combinations. The roller coaster ride I love. As much as I enjoyed dancing with Jose, nothing compares to this. I'm less inhibited. I let my arms move to the music using the styling patterns I learned from all those dreaded hours of practice. It seems a small price to pay for the freedom it gives me to express what I feel.

We dance the night away. He doesn't let me go for the rest of the evening. I'm not sure why. It could be jealousy after watching me dance with Jose. Perhaps it was his plan all along sensing my nervousness and deciding to have me warm up with other dancers to relax me. Maybe he saw something in my dancing that drew him in. Or it could just be that he loves being with me, and he's enjoying himself. I don't care. I'm dancing with Esteban. This is what I want.

Chapter 25 Breakfast at Midnight

When the club closes, a few of us head out for breakfast. We end up at a diner that stays open twenty-four seven. It looks like it hasn't been redecorated since the eighties. There are booths that hug the walls and tables that take up the area in the middle. Fernando picks out a booth, and we all pile in.

I'm the only girl in a group of guys. Esteban, Fernando and Marco are my breakfast partners. Melinda and Marisol were tired and had to work early the next day. The waitress takes our orders, and the guys start talking about the night. After fifteen minutes or so of listening to them talk about who was there, Fernando decides to ask me a question.

"Scarlet, what did you think of the 805?" He asks with a grin.

"I like it. It's a little smaller than La Pura Vida and the Havana Night Club, but I had a good time."

"You visit the Havana Night Club?" Fernando asks.

"Yeah, I go almost every week."

"That's a long way to drive from Lompoc. Do you go with friends?"

"No, I usually go by myself, but I know a lot of people there so I don't mind," I answer.

"You're not afraid of making the drive by yourself at night?" He looks concerned.

"I grew up in Lompoc, so I'm used to the drive. Yeah, it makes me nervous, but the excitement from dancing outweighs my fear," I shrug my shoulders as if to say what can I do.

Fernando looks surprised. I don't think he understands. I wonder if he loves dancing as much as I do. I'm guessing he wouldn't make the drive by himself at night. It wouldn't be worth it.

"Did you find any new dancers to join the group?" Fernando asks Esteban.

"No, how about you guys?" Esteban throws the question back to Fernando and Marco.

"Nope," Marco answers.

"I found one girl who is interested. She said she might come to practice next Thursday," Fernando makes his announcement and his grin widens.

"Is it hard finding people to join the group?" I ask.

"Yes," Esteban answers.

"Why?" I turn towards him. I'm curious.

"Most of the girls take lessons from either Jose in Santa Barbara or Martin in Camarillo. When they come to our practice and see that there aren't many female dancers, they feel uncomfortable. That's why Melinda has been a big help, but she's still learning. The girls like having a woman to teach them how to do styling."

"Oh, it's too bad I don't live here. I'd never miss a class." I don't know what else to say. I can see how hard these guys are working to grow the group. There is nothing I can do to help.

The conversation moves on to other things. Fernando tells us more about the girl who might join the group. It becomes obvious that he has a crush on her. Marco doesn't say much as usual, but Esteban tells us how he sees that Marco is becoming one of the best dancers in Oxnard. Our food comes and we spend the rest of the time laughing, eating, and sharing stories (some true, some exaggerated I'm sure) about our night out dancing.

The next day finds me back in Lompoc with my boys. It feels good to have them home with me. They tell me very little of their time with their dad, and I don't pry, but I can see they're happy to be home. After unpacking and settling back into the apartment, I finally have time to rest.

Sitting with my laptop on my bed, I watch the video the promoter took of me dancing with Jose. I've never seen myself look so happy. This is not the girl I've known myself to be for the past twenty years. There were many times I dreamt of dancing like this with my husband, but we were always too busy with everyday life. If my husband hadn't left me, then I doubt this girl would have ever had a chance to exist.

I wish I could travel back in time to the woman I was the day my husband walked out. I'd kneel beside her on the kitchen floor. I'd hug her and hand her more tissues to blow her nose. We'd watch this video together, eyes open wide, not believing it's really us.

Chapter 26 The Girl in the Mirror

The room is empty, except for me. There are wall to wall mirrors and a glossy wooden gym floor beneath my dance shoes. Music fills the space, passing through my body finding no resistance. I welcome it, invite it, and ask it to take away everything else-my worries, fears, and thoughts.

I have this room to myself for only a little while longer before gym members will start making their way through the corridors. I've been dancing for an hour. One of the perks of having a kind, supportive boss is that she lets me keep a set of keys to the gym and use this dance room in the early morning hours before opening.

I feel a cool wetness on my skin that comes from pushing myself. I try to create that blank space where I let go of the patterns I've practiced so that new ideas can take shape. I watch in the mirror for the unexpected moves that come from this nowhere land. It is the closest thing to real magic I've ever seen. I've been mesmerized by this for the past hour. But all of a sudden, I see something else in the mirror, someone else.

"Mike? How long have you been standing there?" I laugh as I turn around. I realize in my trance I haven't noticed that I wasn't alone. The music must have hidden the sound of the door opening and closing.

"Here? In the room, about five minutes. Outside watching? Maybe a little longer," he teases. Can any girl be mad at him with those green eyes? I'm embarrassed and want to hide, but what can I do? He's standing in front of the door. No escape.

I don't want to look up at his face. I can feel the redness on my cheeks, part from exercise, part from feeling exposed.

"I'm sorry. I couldn't stop watching," Mike confesses. It doesn't sound creepy, but rather apologetic and sincere.

"That's okay. I guess it would be weird seeing someone dancing alone early in the morning. I'd probably watch too," I try to joke my way out of the uncomfortableness.

"No, it's not that. It was beautiful. Really beautiful. I was wrong. Whatever Esteban taught you, whatever you've learned, I can see the difference now. Has he started teaching you again?" Mike asks.

"Yes. Why do you ask? Did you think he would?" I toss a question back to him.

"I knew he would. I could tell by the way he watched you dance with Pablo," Mike smiles, but I'm not sure he wants to. His shoulders seem slouched not his usual perfect posture. His head is tilted slightly downward and his eyes cast towards the wooden floor.

"He didn't want to. I kind of gave him an ultimatum. I threatened to find someone else to teach me."

"Really? You stood up for yourself. And see? It worked," Mike is cheering me on, but his heart doesn't seem in it. "You've improved a lot."

"Do you think so?" I ask. Mike gives a look that tells me he's picked up on my insecurity.

"Well, what do you think?" He asks.

"I must be getting better by now, right?" I throw up my hands in the air to add drama and also to keep it lighthearted so he won't detect anything else.

"I mean it. What do you think?" He asks again.

"I think I am," I answer, but my voice sounds less convincing.

"Scarlet, you don't really see yourself, do you?" Mike's voice becomes a little quieter which draws me in.

"What do you mean?" I ask.

"I mean this room is surrounded by mirrors, and I'm guessing you've been watching yourself dance for an hour by the way you're sweating. How can you not see what is obvious?" His tone isn't mean. It sounds genuinely surprised.

"I don't know. I guess it's because I see myself dance every day. I don't notice the progress."

"No, I think there's more to it," he counters. I know the answer, but I don't want to say it out loud. I wonder if he's guessed it.

Damaged. I feel damaged. I tried my best in my marriage, and my husband left. I didn't see it coming. I must have missed something, a terrible flaw. I watch myself in the mirrors and even though the moves I see look beautiful to me, I wonder if they are flawed in ways my eyes don't detect. Am I missing something? What does Esteban see in Melinda's dancing that he doesn't see in mine?

"Scarlet, if you can't see how beautiful you are in this room filled with mirrors I wonder if you realize how beautiful you are outside these walls. Let me tell you what I see, what the gym members see every day. We see you. Someone who cares about everyone here. I've watched you help so many people. I've watched you teach the exercise machines to women who were afraid to use them. If anyone looks lonely, you're the first one to be their friend. I've seen you teach dance classes with a smile on your face even when you were sick, so you wouldn't disappoint your students." His words make me turn away. He takes a long pause and changes tactics, "Seriously, why do you think I call you the Amazing Scarlet?"

I turn around at his bad joke. He's trying to lighten the weight of his words and make me laugh. I know he's trying to help me, but he doesn't know how close he is to prying into a wound that doesn't heal. He senses that he's going too far, and I see him start to back away towards the door.

"Thanks, Mike," I call out to him. "You're a good friend." He stops and turns toward me one last time when he reaches the door. He looks at me with his green eyes, but doesn't smile.

"Scarlet, do me a favor. Take a good look at the girl in the mirror. Remember what I said. See if you can see her the way I do. It's time for you to really see yourself. Then you won't be so dependent on what others think. You won't need me or anyone else to tell you that you are beautiful. You'll know it." After finishing his words, he offers a smile and walks away.

I bend down to collect my things. My eyes catch my reflection in the mirror. I look so different now. My mind races back in time to what I looked like when my husband left. My eyes were puffy and red from crying. I was at least ten pounds heavier. My hair was always pulled back in a ponytail. I wear my hair down now, especially when I dance. I see it in the mirror falling carefree past my shoulders sweaty from my morning practice.

I stare into my own eyes. Broken. That's what I see. I'm broken. For a second, I feel an overwhelming sadness that threatens to consume me whole. I sit with it until it passes. I look deeper into my own eyes, and I find something else there. It is the brokenness that helps me connect and help so many people. Imperfection is what makes us human and that is what connects us to other humans. This gym is filled with broken people, even if most try to hide it.

I guess that is what Mike sees. The beauty that comes from being broken. It lets whatever was waiting inside you to come out.

Chapter 27 A New Opportunity

"Scarlet, I have the best news! You are not going to believe this," Angie announces as she approaches the front desk at Women4Fitness. I've never seen her this excited. She has the biggest smile. Her whole face is lit up.

"What is it?" I ask.

"You can't say no," Angie starts and spreads her hands out like she is an umpire calling a runner safe. Her words instinctively make me want to say no, but I stay quiet. "I was having lunch with a friend who happens to be the owner of the Grapevine. You know the bar that has country line dancing and West Coast swing. I was sharing with her about how I have a friend who started learning Salsa and that she's dating her handsome teacher." She pauses seeing the horror on my face. "I wasn't going to tell her your name, but she said that she wanted to start having a monthly Salsa Night at the club. She asked me who you were, and you're not going to believe this," Angie takes a deep breath before continuing. "She's taken your dance class before at the gym, and she loves you! She wants you and Esteban to teach a Salsa lesson each month and promote the event!" Angie freezes in excitement and stares at me waiting for my reaction.

"You're right. I can't believe it," I answer.

"You have to do it!" Angie tries to push me in the right direction.

"Let me talk to Esteban. I'm only learning. Esteban would have to be the one to teach the class. I'm guessing he's going to want to do it, but let me talk to him first before I commit to it."

"This is going to be great. I'm so excited!" Angie's voice reminds me of a teenage bestie convincing me to go on a double date.

"Me too. I would love to get this town dancing. This place needs more things to do, and it would be at least one night where I wouldn't have to drive an hour away to dance," I can't help but smile at this thought.

The rest of the day I weigh the pros and cons of helping Esteban teach a dance class. I'm not ready was the predominant thought. There is so much I don't know. I have no desire to teach Salsa. I just have an insatiable craving to learn. Working as a Wellness Coach and Fitness Instructor I put the needs of whoever I'm helping first, but in this one area of my life, Salsa, I am completely selfish. On the other hand, Esteban has been waiting for an opportunity like this. I listen to him talk every night about how he loves to teach people how to dance. Here, away from Oxnard, he might find the students he's been searching for. How can I say no to that?

I can't. I wait for Esteban's nightly phone call to break the news.

"Really? They want us to teach at a club?" There is no mistaking the excitement in his voice. This is something he wants to do.

"Yes, I don't know if we'll get paid for it, or if it's going to even happen for sure. I'll have my friend arrange a time for us to meet with the owner, if you're interested." As much as I am reluctant to do this, I do love the thought of helping him move one step closer to his dream.

"Yes, it doesn't matter if I get paid. This could open doors for us," Esteban replies.

The rest of the conversation was a brainstorm of ideas. How could we make it a success? What could we do to promote it? Which friends from the group might be willing to make the trip? Might there be other places Esteban could teach in the area?

We talked until one in the morning. Exhausted, I hung up the phone and waddled into bed. What have I gotten myself into? I'm not ready for this. I don't know enough.

162

The ghost of myself listens to my troubles as I fall asleep. She considers all of it. No, she thinks, there is no other way.

Chapter 28 It Begins

One week later we sat down with the owner of the Grapevine and agreed to promote the monthly venue and offer a lesson. Since then, Esteban has been busy. Our nightly phone calls include updates on social media marketing strategies, his progress on creating flyers, and my efforts to advertise the event to as many gym members in the little town of Lompoc as I can. One positive side effect is that I haven't heard him mention Melinda's name even once. Esteban has also decided that he should start visiting me on Saturdays, so we can practice.

I'm waiting for him right now. He should be here any minute. I'm not sure what to expect. I'm hoping it will be better. I'm afraid it might be worse. I'm a better dancer. I can do my basic and follow well, but Esteban has high expectations. He wants us to be the best. I've never wanted that. I want something else, something I still don't quite understand.

I warm up in the aerobics room as I wait. When I move, I feel more relaxed. I let the music fill the air. My music, not his. I clear my head and begin to feel what the music asks my body to move. I loosen my arms, my wrists, and unlock my shoulders. Giving them permission to act on their own. I forget that Esteban will be here soon. The worry drifts away. My feet feel not only the wooden floor, but the heartbeat of the rhythm. It carries upward through me as my body starts to play with the different accents it detects, much faster than my head could choreograph.

Then I see him. Esteban walks into the room. He greets me with a hug and kiss, but after that he's all business. He turns off my music and puts on his own. There is no time to waste. We warm up with the basic together.

I can do the basic easily, but I don't seem to hear the beat the same as Esteban. It isn't much of a difference. It is so slight I doubt anyone would notice it. It just feels different. I adjust to his rhythm when I am with him, but when I dance by myself I do it my way. I don't think I am necessarily wrong, because when I dance with other men we seem to match. I think this minor difference is why I had such a hard time learning it in the beginning. Fortunately, it is no longer a problem.

"I have seventy combinations that I teach and have my students memorize in order. I want you to start learning them," he tells me as he takes my hands.

"Seventy?" I ask. That's too many. How will I remember seventy?

"Yes," he answers. Before I can say anything else, he's already taking me through them counting them off.

They are a blur. Some are very similar to each other and since we keep moving I can't get my bearing on any of them. He takes me through the first twenty without stopping. We pause and then he repeats the first twenty combinations again, over and over.

"Can we break it down? There's no way I can remember all of that," I plead.

"You'll learn by practicing," he answers. And then, he turns on the music and we continue on repeating them non-stop.

It could be because I am spinning so much or suffering mental exhaustion from trying to follow and memorize in constant motion, but it feels like one messy goo of moves in my mind. I can't tell one combination from the next even after an hour of practicing.

"I can't remember any of them," I confess. Esteban looks slightly frustrated, but then relaxes.

"I have an idea. I'll be right back," he announces and then leaves the room. I use the opportunity to grab my towel and mop off as much sweat from my body as possible.

Esteban returns and the blood drains down my body to my feet. My brain doesn't want to accept what my eyes see. He's brought Mike with him. Mike has a big grin and is trying not to laugh. I must look like a mess. Esteban hasn't released a drop of sweat, and I look like I've just come from a swim class.

"Scarlet, give him your phone. He's going to record this for you, so you can memorize the combinations." Esteban seems happy with his plan.

"What?" I hear myself say before I've realized I've said anything out loud. Mike covers his mouth to hide his laughing.

"He's going to record us," Esteban repeats the instructions as he sets up the music to play.

I give Mike my phone. I don't want to look him in the eye.

"Thanks for doing this, Mike," I tell him even though I don't really want him to capture me looking like a sweaty Raggedy Ann doll who's going to be tossed around in every direction.

"Of course, I wouldn't miss this for the world." He leans in closer as he adds, "When I saw him asking people, I volunteered my services." And although I wouldn't believe it possible, his grin grows even wider.

Esteban doesn't give us time for chit chat. He's already grabbed both of my hands and has me moving. He calls out the combinations over the music like a football coach shouting directions to his players. Forget doing the moves slowly. Who needs that, right? I have no choice but to follow as best as I can, fully aware that Mike is watching my every move. When I spin I can feel the sweat fly off my hair. What a beautiful look! The look of utter surprise (or despair) as I try to anticipate all the twists and turns Esteban springs upon me captured forever on video.

I'd like to suggest recording these moves again slowly without the music, but that would require Mike to stay with us even longer. I'd rather not.

At the end of the sequence, Esteban turns off the music and walks over to Mike.

"Thanks for doing this," Esteban tells him as he takes back the phone and hands it to me. "Now memorize the combinations this week so we can start the next twenty on Saturday," Esteban instructs me without laughing. He's not kidding. He's being serious.

I wonder if Mike's face is mirroring my own, because he looks how I feel. That's impossible! If I read Mike's expression correctly, it's telling me to say something. Speak up! That is just too much. But, I can't. Instead, I redirect the focus.

"Hey, Mike. Thanks for helping us. We're hosting a Salsa Night at the Grapevine a month from now. Would you do me a big favor and advertise it in your classes?"

"Of course," he pauses before adding on, "and I'll even see if Pablo can come." Mike smiles as he says these last few words and playfully throws a soft punch to my upper arm before turning away and exiting the room. Esteban's body stiffens, but he doesn't say anything.

"Do you want to keep going?" I ask.

"No, I think that's enough practice for today. Let's grab some lunch. Afterwards, we'll start putting up flyers." Esteban packs up the music, and I head to the locker room to see if I can make myself look normal again.

After lunch, we spend the rest of the day searching for places to hang flyers. As we walk about, we have lots of time to brainstorm ideas on how to make the Salsa Night a success. Then a thought pops into my head out of nowhere.

"Esteban, I want to go dancing in LA. Will you take me?" I can't imagine anything else I would rather do than go dancing with Esteban in LA, just the two of us. A real date. Some place I've never been, doing something I truly love.

"One day," Esteban smiles as he hands me a flyer to tape on a board.

"I want to go one day soon," I smile back trying to use my persuasive powers.

"You're not ready," he counters.

"It makes no difference to me if I'm a good dancer, as long as I go with you. I just want to see what it's like. I'm curious."

"No, not until you're ready. Trust me, it will be so much better if you're a strong dancer," he answers as we walk towards another community board. I choose not to pursue it further at the moment. I do plan to revisit the topic again soon. I've already decided I'm going to go.

We spend a couple of hours putting out posters. Esteban still has plenty left for us to use for advertisement next Saturday. Afterwards, we visit our favorite local ice cream shop. We're regulars. They know us.

This is when I like him best. Relaxed. He shares his vision of having his own dance team, but instead of being serious he laughs and smiles. I never get bored talking to him, even though we talk for hours every night. How could I? I've never met anyone who has so many hopes and dreams.

Chapter 29 LA Dreams

The next few weeks follow a predictable pattern. I teach my classes, work, advertise our event, take care of my boys, try to memorize the combinations (which don't stick), and have a lesson on Saturday with Esteban. Every night my body crawls to bed exhausted.

Late at night before I drift to sleep, I wonder what it would be like to take lessons with Luis Chavez. Esteban has shared with me what it was like to be his student. It has become my favorite bed time story. I can almost feel myself on the dance floor waiting for the lesson to begin.

My imagination has reconstructed the dance studio from the details I've gathered from Esteban. The front wall has large mirrors that cover the length of the room. Above the mirrors, there is a strip of wall painted a light lavender color, and written in dark grey cursive letters the phrase, "Practice Makes Perfect."

In my dream scene, I'm never in the front row, but rather in the back somewhere. Luis is up front and center. The girl with long red hair is standing to his right. I watch and follow trying my best to look like them. Whether I'm succeeding or not, I feel happy. It's like I'm meant to be there. Esteban is never with me in this dream. I brave the class solo.

My dreams invade my thoughts when I drive to the Havana Night Club. I see myself dancing in a club in LA. This time Esteban is with me. He's spinning me around him. I can feel the frenzy of the dancers surrounding us, doing moves I've never seen before.

I've asked Cindy what it's like dancing in LA. Her answer is always the same, "Come with me."

I've been bugging Esteban to take me. I mention it in our nightly calls and when he visits for our lesson. He answers with, "I'm too busy to go to LA right now. Besides, you need to stay focused on our upcoming Salsa Night."

The more he tells me that, the more I dream of LA.

Chapter 30 The Grand Opening

I can't relax. Tonight is the night. I've practiced all I could. I've told everyone about our Salsa Night from students, friends, co-workers, gym members, to every stranger encountered in the grocery store. There is nothing left to do, except feel afraid.

I feel like a fraud. I haven't been dancing long enough to be teaching. I've been passing out flyers for a month now that has my name listed as a "Salsa Instructor." That's not true. Why did Esteban have to put my name on the flyer? I wish I could cross it out with a black marker and scribble "Helper" instead. Teacher is too weighty a word. It comes with expectations. Ones I can't possibly meet since I've only started dancing. I've tried to tell this to Esteban, but he says not to worry. I'll learn faster if I teach. I don't think so.

My friend Cindy told me that people at the Havana Night Club have been asking her about me and the new Salsa Night. I worry they are watching me, judging me. Asking, "Who does she think she is?"

Esteban said that I should get used to it. People talk behind his back all the time. Don't let it bother me. Yeah, right.

My boys are already settled at Grandma's so I have plenty of time to get myself ready. I'm wearing my favorite red dress with silver heels. The dress is sleeveless and hugs my torso. The bottom of the dress flairs out when I spin, but has enough weight to keep it from flying too high. I've tested it out in the mirror dozens of times to make sure it works with my dance moves.

I've been careful to eat enough so I have energy but not so much that I would feel sluggish. I've been drinking plenty of water and even skipped working out yesterday to make sure my muscles are fresh. My body is in peak condition. I've controlled every possible detail that I can, but the wildcard remains Esteban.

When I dance with Esteban, he always improvises. It's why I love dancing with him. Although he has me trying to memorize his seventy combinations (which I can't seem to do), he changes them all the time. It took me a while to realize that he was indeed switching up the moves like my mother used to do when I was five and learning hula. I questioned him one day during practice.

"Esteban, I don't remember this combination ending that way last time. It seems different," I told him after we'd been practicing for an hour. I was getting frustrated because I was finding it impossible to memorize the combinations.

"That's because I add variations to keep it interesting. It also protects against other Salseros trying to copy my moves," he answered.

"Wait, you're changing the combinations on purpose?" I asked. I couldn't believe it. Why have me try to memorize the moves if you're just going to change them?

"Yes," Esteban replied as he tried to get me moving again.

"Wait," I stopped him. "How am I supposed to memorize the combinations?"

"Just memorize the base and follow the rest," Esteban answered and before I knew it I was spinning again. My body was spinning because it was being lead to and my head was spinning try to unwind Esteban's logic.

That conversation took place about two weeks ago. I've accepted my fate. Esteban is not going to change, and I probably wouldn't enjoy dancing with him if he did.

My fear is that he won't hold back during the lesson. I'm worried he'll throw in something I won't know how to follow and I will look like the inexperienced dancer that I am. As I apply my make up, I pray this doesn't happen.

When I arrive at the Grapevine, I am the first one there. This gives me extra time to sit in my car and think. I consult with the ghost of myself. I imagine her sitting next to me wearing the same outfit, the same hairdo, another version of myself.

"I'm scared," I tell her.

"I know," she answers.

"Well, what do you think? Say something to make me feel better," my thoughts feel short and desperate.

"I can't," she replies.

I turn towards her in my mind, "Why?"

She hesitates. "I'm worried too," the ghost whispers back.

"What?" I want to find out more, but I see Esteban's caravan pull up alongside me in the parking lot.

Esteban's Sentra parks next to mine. I look out my window and see Melinda looking back at me. Startled, I try to recover quickly and give a polite wave and smile. Inside, I feel weak. Esteban never mentioned that he was bringing Melinda. Marco waves to me from the back seat.

Driving the second car is Fernando. I watch as Marisol and three men I don't recognize emerge from the vehicle. The Jolly Green Giant steps out and stretches his arms wide. I may not be happy to see Melinda, but at least Esteban brought dancers.

Esteban greets me with a hug and kiss, "Are you ready?"

"As ready as I can be," I answer trying to sound hopeful instead of terrified.

I give a round of hugs to everyone, including Melinda. We head inside to set up the event. The Grapevine has hired its own deejay so Esteban talks to him about music for the lesson. I double check my hair and makeup in the bathroom. People should start coming in any minute now. I wonder how many of my friends will actually show.

The deejay puts on a Salsa tune. The place feels more friendly. My shoulders start to relax. Melinda and the Jolly Green Giant take the dance floor followed by Marisol and one of the new guys. Marco walks over to me and extends his hand.

You couldn't ask for a better dance floor. The place has the feel of a country barn, but with a dance floor carved in heaven, spacious and smooth, a dancer's dream. Wooden tables and chairs line up against the walls giving the dancers center stage.

Dancing makes me forget what's coming next, Melinda's presence, and my fears. I let Marco lead me. I begin to believe that maybe tonight might turn out wonderful. As one song blends into the next, I start to notice the Grapevine filling with guests. I see some of my students and friends among the growing crowd, and there are many others that I don't know. It warms my heart when I see Mike in the doorway.

I rush over to Mike to say hello.

"I can't believe you're here," I say as I give him a hug. "You're going to take the lesson?"

"Yes, me and my two left feet," he laughs. "I'm sorry. Pablo couldn't make it. He wanted to be here, but he had to work. He promised to come to one in the future."

"That's okay. I have you. The women are going to love you," I can't help but smile seeing him grimace at the thought. "I have to get ready for the lesson. I'll catch up with you after."

I try to say hello to as many friends as I can while making my way to Esteban. It's a good turnout. The place is packed. I can feel the worries return, but I choose to ignore them.

"Esteban, are you ready?" I ask as I approach.

"Scarlet," he looks a little pale, "I'm nervous."

"You're nervous?" I wasn't expecting this. He's been so excited. I don't think he ever mentioned being nervous.

"I've never taught so many people at once," he shares.

I don't know why it never occurred to me before. I'm used to teaching large crowds of people in my aerobics classes. I've even lead classes at fundraisers with over a hundred people. Esteban has only taught small groups. This would be overwhelming.

"That's okay. You'll feel better once you start moving. Let me introduce us. Then I'll let you take over leading the warm up. Afterwards, you'll feel better about talking. Trust me. Once you start moving, it will be easier," I give him a kiss on the cheek. I decide it's better to get started right away so he doesn't have time to worry more. I grab the microphone.

"Hello everyone! Thanks for coming out to our first Salsa Night at the Grapevine! Can I have everyone here for the lesson come out to the dance floor. Don't be shy. This is our first Salsa Night, so we have a lot of beginners here. Bring both of your left feet with you, and we'll get you dancing." I hear some chuckles from the crowd and see the dance floor filling up. I count at least three rows of people. Not bad for our first night.

"My name is Scarlet, and this here is Esteban. He will be teaching you tonight. We're going to play some music to warm up and have fun. It's just to loosen the body and give you an idea of some of the moves we'll be teaching. After the song, we will break down the moves step by step so that you can learn." I signal the deejay to play the music and smile at Esteban. He looks a little scared, but he's still breathing. That's a good sign.

I can see him start to relax as he moves. He even starts to smile. He begins with the basic and then transitions into side to side steps. I like that he's keeping it simple. I watch the crowd and see that most are beginners. They're laughing at themselves trying Salsa for the first time and looking to their friends for support. This is a forgiving crowd with good humor.

When the song ends, Esteban gets his voice back and breaks down the steps slowly. I'm glad he isn't teaching them the way he teaches me. They'd never survive. Tonight, he's doing a good job of making it easy to learn. This goes on for the first hour. Teaching the basic steps and playing the music to practice.

"Okay, take a quick break and then come back for partner work," Esteban announces to the crowd.

Esteban turns towards me, "Thank you, Scarlet. There's no way I could have done this without you." He gives me a hug and kiss before walking over towards the deejay.

I head over to Mike. I am curious what he thought about the first half.

"How do you think it's going?" I ask.

"You guys are doing a good job. People seem to be having fun and catching on," Mike tells me. I study his face. I believe he's telling the truth. He isn't sugarcoating it.

"Okay, I was feeling kind of nervous about this whole thing. I guess I better get back. We'll be starting the partner work next. That's the part I'm most worried about," I hear my voice weaken at the end.

"Don't worry. You'll do fine. You should be more worried about me falling down," he laughs.

"If you do, you'll have at least a dozen girls rush over to rescue you. The women are very happy to have you here. Thanks again for

176

coming," I leave him with those last words and head back to Esteban.

"Ready for part two?" I ask Esteban as I place my hand on his shoulder.

"Ready," he states as he turns back to the crowd.

"Okay, time for partner work. I want the ladies to line up on this side with Scarlet, and the men to form a line opposite them. Good. Now let me show you how to hold her hands," Esteban demonstrates using me as his assistant.

We follow this pattern of teaching, showing, and having them follow. Esteban has them rotating partners often so everyone gets to know each other. There is a nice feel of camaraderie. He's sticking to our plan.

"Now, I'm going to demonstrate what you can do with a little practice," Esteban announces. This is the part I'm nervous about. Freestyle dancing with him in front of everyone. We've been practicing this each week. I've been working so hard memorizing the confusing combinations so I won't embarrass us. I pray he doesn't do anything crazy.

Esteban motions to Melinda to join him. I'm stunned. The deejay turns on the music. They begin to dance. He takes her through the combinations, adding dips that I haven't learned yet. I doubt my body could even bend as far as hers. I remember the video we watched at my apartment on Thanksgiving of Luis dancing. The girl doing acrobatics that I am not capable of, the look on Esteban's face of wanting to dance like that one day. The realization that given my flexibility it's not a possibility for me. I feel like a fool. To be teaching the class, and then have another girl perform in my place. Showing everyone I really am a fraud. My name shouldn't be on the poster as an instructor. Hell, I never wanted to be a labeled as an instructor. And yet, right now, I feel betrayed. It should be me out there, even if I were to screw up. It should be me. I can feel the heat of the tears ready to spill out. I slowly move back through the crowd towards the door. Everyone is watching them dance. I sneak out before embarrassing myself.

I feel the tears drip down my cheeks. I can't stop it. I make my way around the building to the very back, hoping I won't get mugged. I don't want anyone to see me. I wipe the tears and try to regain control of my emotions.

"Scarlet, are you okay," Mike's voice, soft and soothing, calls to me. I feel him standing behind me before I even turn around. I wipe my face one last time before facing him.

"No, I'm not," I confess. What would be the point of lying? It's bad enough I'm crying. Lying on top of it would be pathetic.

"I thought you could use a friend, and I didn't want to have you back here alone."

"Thanks," I can't help but sniffle with my plugged nose, "it probably isn't the safest place to hang out by myself."

"You were surprised that he danced with the other girl," Mike states the obvious. Might as well save time and be direct.

"Yes," I answer. "It wasn't what we had planned."

"Why didn't he dance with you? I'm sorry, Scarlet, but you move better than her," Mike says it like he sees it. I read in his body language that he believes what he has said. He's looking me in the eye.

"I can't do the dips that she can," I feel another tear escape down my face. "For whatever reason or sick joke of the universe, my lower body isn't flexible. My arms, shoulders, rib cage are very flexible, but past the waist, no. I've never been able to do the things most women can when it comes to back bends and touching their toes. If I could fix it, I would. This is just the way my body is designed. There is only so much I can do without hurting myself."

178

"I understand," he sighs. I know he understands. As a fitness instructor, I know he is fully aware of what I'm saying. We have to work with what we have and be grateful for it. Push to the point of injury long enough and you're setting yourself up for a lifetime of pain. It's not worth it.

"I know you do," I smile. I'm still miserable, but it feels good to be understood. I feel relief at getting my feelings out into the night air and having someone listen. "Esteban chose to dance with Melinda, because she can do things with her body that I can't."

Mike is quiet for a while. I wait for him to say something.

"Scarlet, can I ask you a question?"

"Sure," I answer.

"What would you have done if things were reversed?" He asks.

"What?" I'm confused.

"Say you were teaching the class, and Esteban was helping you. He's helping you put out flyers, practicing endless hours, memorizing insane combinations, doing his best to make your dream come true. He's invited every friend he has to come out and support your Salsa Night," as Mike says this my eyes water and get blurry. He continues on, "Would you dance with him and modify the moves to make him look good too or would you choose to dance with Pablo just so you could look better?"

"I would dance with Esteban," I answer.

"I know you would," Mike replies. "I've told you before. You two dance for different reasons. I bet when we return he will still be dancing. Have you asked yourself why he isn't looking for you right now?"

"He probably can't find me," I give a little laugh thinking of hanging out in the back alley on our Grand Opening.

"Well, if you were my girlfriend I wouldn't have stopped looking," Mike softly touches the side of my face to get me to look at him. As soon as I do, he removes his hand so I won't feel afraid that he's stepping beyond friendship.

"Look, we are not going to let those two get the best of you. The whole town has come out to support your Salsa Night. I can't fix anything that Esteban's done, but maybe I can do something to distract you and make it a little easier for you to go back in there," Mike says as his lips form a slight smile.

"What?"

"Scarlet, will you dance with me?"

Chapter 31 And the Show Goes On

As we walk through the open doors of the Grapevine, I see my friend Cindy. I give her a hug before heading out to the dance floor with Mike.

Mike looks nervous, but he's really doing it. He's taking me out for a dance. I catch jealous glances from more than a few women that I recognize from his boot camp class. The music begins and he takes my hands in his and looks at me with his green eyes. His hands are warm, and even though we are just friends, I do feel like melting. I am only human.

He moves back and forth with the Salsa basic. He isn't clumsy this time, and he doesn't have a death grip. In fact, it feels like I'm holding hands with someone else I know. I give him the weight of my hands, nothing more nothing less. Before I can say anything, he takes me for a double spin and into a cross body lead. After that, he keeps me moving.

The combinations are simple, but they are varied and the leads are clear. I can't believe it. We're actually dancing. His two left feet are working together. I find myself laughing and smiling. He has a goofy grin on his face. I guess he learned that too. The same goofy grin that puts me at ease when I dance. Reminding me this is just for fun.

Mike lets me go so we can dance on our own, and to my surprise, he shows off some footwork. His upper body is stiff, but his feet are moving on beat. After impressing me, he draws me back in. At the end of the song, he pulls me away and spins me towards him taking me into a quick dip and bringing me up into his arms with my hair flying onto his shoulders.

"You've learned to dance! How?" I ask, although I already know the answer.

"You're not the only one taking lessons," he replies as he lifts his chin slightly and raises a brow.

"Pablo taught you. I recognized it the minute you took my hands."

"Yes, Pablo, and his sister, Lupe, has been nice enough to practice with me," Mike answers. I hear something in his voice when he mentions Lupe's name. Maybe I'm just imagining it?

"Looks like I'm going to have to share you with all the women tonight. They know you can dance now. There will be no escaping them," I love to see the torment my words cause him. The expression of distaste that slides across his face.

"Well, I better say goodbye now, because the first chance I get to sneak away I will," he gives me one more hug. "Try to enjoy tonight, dance with as many men as you can. Remember, your friends came here to support you. Everything else you can figure out tomorrow, okay?"

"Yes, that is my plan," and with those parting words a girl interrupts and drags Mike back out on the floor. I take no more than two steps and a guy I recognize from Santa Barbara takes me back out as well.

I spend the rest of the night dancing non-stop. I don't expect Esteban to ask me to dance. Our plan is to dance with people who have no one to dance with, especially the beginners. We want everyone to have a good time and not feel left out. Still, I keep an eye out for where he is dancing so I can avoid him in between songs. I don't know what to say to him yet, so it's best not to say anything.

Time passes quickly, and somewhere towards the end of the night, Cindy pulls me aside to say goodbye. I walk with her outside.

"Thanks for coming," I tell her as I give her a hug.

"Scarlet, can I ask you something?"

"Sure, what is it?"

"Are you okay? You don't seem like yourself tonight. I noticed you didn't dance with Esteban, or even talk to him the whole night," Cindy watches my expression trying to read me.

"I'm all right. I'd be happier if I could go dancing in LA," I joke with her trying to avoid her real question.

"Then come with me!" She says exhausted of repeating this phrase.

"I want to, but for some reason, I've always imagined going with Esteban the first time. I'm not a good dancer yet, and at least with him I'd be on the dance floor. Otherwise, I don't think anyone would want to dance with me since I'm a beginner." In my mind, every LA dancer is an expert. On some level, I know that's unrealistic, but going without Esteban intimidates me.

"What makes you think that? Yeah, you have some really good dancers there, but you find all levels. And Scarlet, you can hold your own on the dance floor. Men will want to dance with you," Cindy counters. After a pause, she continues on, "Don't wait for Esteban. He doesn't wait for you. I saw him dancing at El Tigre last week with Melinda."

"What?" Her words hit me like a truck.

"Yes," her eyes start to water and I can tell it's hard for her to spit the words out. "Look, I was going to tell you the next time you came to Santa Barbara. I didn't want to tell you over the phone or even here, but hearing you talk of LA so much and then seeing Melinda here tonight. Well, I think you should know."

"What did you see?" I ask. This time I want details. I'm ready to hear whatever she has to say.

"I didn't see them kiss or do anything romantic together, but it was just the two of them. They danced together all night. I'm sorry, Scarlet. I don't understand why he would take her to LA instead of you. And don't let him tell you it's because you can't dance, that's bullshit!" I can see the anger in her face. The narrowing of her eyes and straight-lined mouth. The same anger I have rising up in myself.

"Thanks for telling me. I know it wasn't easy," I give her a hug. "I'm going to talk to Esteban. Be safe driving home. I know what it's like making that drive by yourself late at night. Don't worry about me. I'll be okay." I keep my voice calm even though inside my head is pounding. Cindy gives me one last hug and heads out. I imagine she needs the drive home to recover. It's hard telling someone the truth, especially one they need to hear. Like Mike, she is a dear friend.

I take my time walking back into the club. I breathe, but this time I don't try to soothe my rage. How many times have I asked him to take me to LA? He was too busy. That was his answer. Showing off with Melinda here in front of all my friends that came out to support us. This conversation isn't going to wait. It's going to happen now.

Chapter 32 I've Had It

I walk back into the Grapevine. It's almost the closing hour. The dance floor has only three couples, one pair being Esteban and Melinda. I should have guessed. I grab my things and pack them in my car. My mind is already made up.

I re-enter the club and wait for the song to end. I feel hot. My blood is boiling inside me, but I will myself to stay calm. I have to find out if he is intentionally lying to me. I have to be sure. The song finishes with Esteban taking Melinda into a low dip. All the onlookers love it, except me.

"There you are," I say as I walk up to him. "I haven't danced with you all night."

"Do you want to dance now?" He asks.

"No, I'd like to talk to you outside," I take his hand and lead him out front.

"Okay, but only for a moment. The deejay is about to leave, and I need to talk to him about next time," Esteban grudgingly follows me out.

"This won't take long," I laugh. "You know I've worked really hard for this, right?"

"Yes," he says and smiles. "I think it was a big success."

"Me too," I tell him. "So I think I've earned my trip to LA for a night out dancing. What do you think?"

"Oh, Scarlet. I'm too busy, and money is tight. I can't afford it right now. I've been spending money on the flyers and advertising," he answers. I notice he doesn't meet my eyes.

"Oh, come on. When was the last time you went to LA?" I probe further.

"I don't know. At least six months ago, before I met you," he tells me. He still doesn't look at me directly. My heart sinks. I know what I have to do.

"Esteban, you hurt my feelings when you danced with Melinda instead of me during the lesson. It embarrassed me in front of my friends. I'm listed as an instructor on the flyer. Why would you do that?"

"I didn't think it was a big deal. I thought I'd take some of the pressure off of you by having her dance instead. I know you were worried about it. Does it really matter?" He looks surprised.

"Yes, it matters. I worked really hard so I wouldn't embarrass us. At the last minute, you chose to dance with her. You brought her here so you could show off, and my feelings didn't matter to you at all. I don't want to do this anymore. I'm going to step down from teaching the class with you. Melinda can take my place. It's obvious that you prefer her. You tell me over and over again how great of a dancer she is," I hear my voice starting to rise in pitch. I can't hold back the anger.

"Wait a minute, Scarlet. This isn't like you. Where is this coming from?" Esteban tries to hold my hand to calm me. I pull away. I have to finish this.

The deejay interrupts us, "Bye guys!" He waves as he heads out to his car.

"Hold on a minute. I want to talk to you about next time. Wait just a second, okay?" Esteban calls out to him.

"Sure, but it will have to be quick. I have a long drive back home," he answers.

"Scarlet, just give me a minute and we'll talk some more," he tells me. He doesn't care about me. All he cares about is his dance company and this Salsa Night.

"Don't bother. I know you went to LA with Melinda," I lay it out there.

"What?" Esteban looks like I slapped his face.

"Cindy saw the two of you. How could you take someone else after I've only asked you a million times? And then, you lie about it to my face! I'm done. You can have this event with Melinda. I won't take it away from you. I'll tell the owner that I'm just busy. I wish you luck with it. But as for me? Leave me alone." And with that, I start to walk away.

"No, you have it all wrong!" He tries to step in front of me, to get me to listen.

"Hey, dude!" The deejay calls out, "I got to go. I'll catch up with you next time, okay?"

"No, wait. I'm coming!" Esteban heads towards him. "Scarlet, please, I'm begging you. Wait here. I need to get his phone number. I'll be right back. You don't know the whole story. Please stay here, okay? I can explain. There is something you don't know." And with those words, he runs over to the deejay.

I stay put until I see him travel to the other side of the parking lot. With my keys in hand, my gear packed and my final words spoken, I leave.

I drive home with my vision blurred from tears. I keep wiping them, but they keep coming back. The ghost of myself stays silent. I know she wants to tell me something.

"What is it?" I finally ask.

"Don't you want to know?" She turns towards me.

"Know what?"

"What he would have said if you had stayed," she looks sad.

"No," I answer.

Chapter 33 An Unexpected Offer

I turned off my phone before heading into my apartment. The next day I bought a new phone and changed my number. Its extreme. I know its extreme, but I'm giving myself a break. My coping abilities are already taxed from the divorce. Ending my relationship with Esteban is more than I can deal with. I need space to clear my head and think straight. The last thing I want to be doing is checking my phone to see if he calls or not.

I'm skipping the Havana Night Club this week. My heart isn't in it.

I haven't stopped practicing. Actually, I find myself practicing more. It's the only time the pain eases. I practice everything he taught me, and I create new steps of my own. Sometimes, memories of him surface, but while I'm dancing they don't hurt. The movement keeps me from staying stuck in anything too painful.

My work saves me during the day. Every hour someone shares with me their dream of changing their life. I listen to them and help coach them toward their goal. It feels good to be useful, even if my life is falling apart.

Mike asked me about Esteban, but I told him I wasn't ready to talk about it. I wonder what my face must have looked like when I said the words out loud, because he didn't pry. He quietly walked away and hasn't brought it up since.

I hide what I feel around my boys. They've been through enough. My sons are the reason I keep going, one foot in front of the other, one heartbreak after another. We have our evening routine of sharing about our day, homework, and an occasional movie night at home.

Bed time is the worst. I miss hearing his voice. I miss having someone who asks what I want out of life. The excitement in his voice as he plans for the future. Night time is when I cry. Quiet tears so my boys won't hear. I can't believe he lied to me. How could I have been such a fool?

Most of my tears are for Esteban, but some are leftover from the divorce. Loss after loss. Crawling into bed alone. Remembering better. Wondering where it went wrong, and why I didn't see it coming.

This is where I was when I received a text from my ex-husband. Lying in bed with my cheeks wet with tears, I read his message. He asked if I could bring the boys to LA for the weekend. His car is in bad shape, and he's not able to make the drive. He misses them. Gary makes me an offer I can't refuse. If I drive the boys down on Saturday, he'll pay for a hotel room for me. Then I can take the boys back home with me on Sunday. I'd be able to spend one night alone in LA.

El Tigre has Salsa dancing on Saturdays. I wipe my wet face, blow my nose, and write back telling him I'll do it.

Chapter 34 A Dream Come True

We cruise along the Pacific Coast Highway listening to music handpicked by my teenager. According to him, his playlist is much better than mine. My little guy has the backseat to himself. The ocean does its magic thing on my right, being its incredible self even on an ordinary day. No matter how bad I feel on the inside, the ocean reminds me that God must be out there somewhere.

We eventually pull up to my ex-husband's place, a new house with a new wife. He's already replaced everything I've lost. And me? My life is a mess. Next month is my birthday. I'll be forty-one. Instead of having stability, I have nothing.

No. That's not true, something inside me speaks up. You have your two boys. I come back to myself. I take a breath and let go of the negativity that has me in a stranglehold. I wish my ex-husband well, although I also wish I'd never have to see or talk to him again. I'm going to use whatever resources I have to build a better life for myself, not waste it thinking about him. He is no longer a part of my life. Whether he is happy or sad doesn't affect me. So, I choose to wish him happiness. I reason, if nothing else, it's energy efficient.

After giving hugs and kisses, my sons walk up to their father's front door. They ring the bell, wave goodbye, and in the next moment they are gone. I miss them already.

I spend the rest of the day preparing for my night out. I drive by El Tigre so I won't get lost at night, check into my hotel, unpack, take a nap, and grab some dinner.

The hotel is in a nice area, so I'm not scared. The room is simple and clean. What more could I need? It has the comfiest pillows I've ever felt. If only I could take one home with me. I know I will spend the rest of my life hoping to find these pillows again. The bedspread is a mixture of colors, unsuccessfully blending shades of pink and purple. The watercolor on the opposite wall looks like it was chosen to match the bed. It has no discernable subject. Abstract. Very abstract. It doesn't matter. I won't see this room again until the early morning hours, when all I'll care about is that soft pillow.

I bought a new dress. Red, of course. It has a short hemline and has fringes made of sheer fabric which flare when I spin. As I dress for the night, I play the TV in the background. I miss my boys. The voices from the television make me feel less lonely.

I'm nervous going to the club by myself. I could have invited Cindy, but for some reason I didn't feel like it. Part of me wants silence and stillness to sort things out. And part of me wants a solo adventure with maybe a tad of fear to distract me from thinking about Esteban.

One troublesome thought nags at me. Esteban says I'm not ready to dance in LA. I've heard his voice throughout the day. You need to wait. You need to practice more first. As I add the finishing touches to my hair and makeup, I finally answer him. I don't care. I'm going anyways. When will I ever have the chance to do this again? If they don't ask me to dance, I'll ask them. In fact, I'll ask the best dancer I see. What will he do? Say no? I doubt it. With that last thought, I grab my keys and leave.

El Tigre is crowded by the time I arrive. It's darker than the other clubs I've visited. On stage there is a live band playing. The dancers feed off their energy. To my left is the bar with a row of men standing drinks in hand. The dance floor is in the center. The bystanders watch on the outskirts. People talk to each other, but most of us watch the dancing couples.

The couple in front of me is quite good. They are doing moves I haven't seen used before in Salsa. The moves aren't exactly original, but rather recycled from the eighties with an updated style making it more modern, old meets new. Here, anything goes as long as it's on beat. This seems to be the unspoken rule as I look around the club. I recognize moves borrowed from hip hop, belly dancing, ballet, and even tap dancing.

The best dancers have their own style. I see only a handful of those, maybe five or six couples. Cindy is right. There is a mix of levels. I see beginners, intermediates, and never danced a day in my lifers. I should have no problem fitting in.

But, I am not here to fit in. Tonight, I want the chance to dance with some of the best. "Why not?" The ghost of myself speaks up. "What else did we come here for?"

"Would you like to dance?" A man interrupts my thoughts. He's at least a decade younger than me, thin-framed, dark skinned, and about four inches taller. His long sleeve shirt is worn untucked with his sleeves rolled up. Gently, he takes my hand and leads me to the floor.

I feel like I'm dancing with Michael Jackson. That is the best way I can describe it. If Michael danced Salsa, I'm sure this is what it would look like. His body picks up nuances in the music that everyone else misses. Hidden accents that allow him to express more than others. He hits the beats, but the way he gets there is varied depending on the feel of the music. I have to listen to his hands. I have to follow exactly to create the effect he's after. I also have to loosen my body so the music moves through me the way it moves through him. To see his vision of the music I have to be a blank slate. I give him only the weight of my hands so he is free to let me into his world. When the song is over I wonder if I will ever be able to dance his way again. Heaven on loan for only a song. I give him a hug and thank him before we part ways.

"Scarlet?" I hear a voice I recognize behind me. Turning around, I see Pablo. I give him a hug. It feels good to see a friend.

"You finally made it to LA. Why didn't you call me?"

"It was a last minute decision," I answer.

"Did you come by yourself?" He asks.

"Yes," I say and watch the worried expression on his face.

"You're not driving all the way back to Lompoc tonight. Are you?"

"No, I have a hotel room," I calm his worries.

"Okay, promise me that you'll let me walk you to your car tonight. Don't leave the club without me." He seems a little fatherly, but it sounds like a good plan to me.

"I promise," I answer feeling relieved.

"Let me introduce you to some people," he takes me around to several of his friends, most of them men. They each take turns taking me on the floor. Pablo also points out some of the best dancers in the club. Two of them grab my attention.

The first is a woman who has blonde hair, longer than mine. Hers travels all the way down to her waist and is pulled back into a low pony tail. She has a dancer's body, slender and toned. Her style is a mixture of Salsa and ballroom. Her footwork is different from other women. Her feet are placed precisely. Her toes point out on each step. If there was a word stamped on her forehead it would say, "Class." I don't know how else to explain it. There is a polish and elegance that I see in no other dancer here. Pablo tells me her name is Sonya Lexington. She is a World Champion, and the current dance partner of Luis Chavez.

The second dancer that stands out is a man. He looks to be my age. Like Sonya, he has a precision that other dancers lack. What I see in him is intensity. He isn't as graceful as Sonya, but he has his partner flowing in quick combinations with dramatic pauses, dips, and even a move called the Tornado. The Tornado starts with the girl spinning close to the floor more times than I can count and slowly she makes her way up to standing all the time being turned around at top speed. This is the first time I've seen it done at a club.

Pablo tells me the man is Hector Ramos, a five-time World Champion.

I only dance with Pablo once. I think he understands my desire to sample as many dancers as I can. One dance blends into the next, until I muster the courage to do what I want most. I ask Hector Ramos for a dance. Brave, foolish, unheard of, probably all of the above, but I don't live in LA and I'm not sure I'll ever venture out this far again.

I've been watching him all night He's seems nice. I've seen him dance with most of the women in the club, whether they are beginners or advanced. Afterwards, he hands him his business card so I guess he's advertising his classes. This makes it a little easier for me to be so forward. He's kind enough to say yes and escorts me on to the floor.

He is only a few inches taller than me but his posture is perfect. It makes me stand taller. I realize I've been slouching throughout most of the night, and so have my partners. He starts with us in a closed frame which makes me place my hand on his shoulder as we begin with the basic. This makes sense. He has more control over me this way. I can feel when he wants me to move. Once he trusts me to keep the beat with the basic he switches to an open frame. Hector begins with simple spins and cross body leads to feel out what I am capable of following.

I lose track of what we do after that. I can't believe I am dancing with a champion. He's forgiving of my mistakes and keeps a smile on his face. I respect that he is willing to dance with everyone, not just the best dancers. Hector lets me go so we can freestyle. I give into the moment and just enjoy myself. My body listens to whatever the music tells me to do. I know I'll never remember what steps I did. They will be lost to me as soon as he grabs my hands again. I see him though with triple spins and intricate footwork that pleases the crowd. We come together again and the song ends. I'm so grateful he didn't try to dip me. My guess is that he sensed I couldn't do it. Smart guy.

"I'm Hector. What's your name?"

"Scarlet. Thanks for dancing with me. That was great," I give him a hug.

"You're a pretty good dancer. I can teach you even more. Here's my card. Check out the website. It has all my classes," he hands me his card.

"Thank you," I take it like its gold, or more like a dream. I wish I could take his classes, but inside I know it's not possible. There is so much that I could learn.

"Are you on Facebook?" He asks.

"Yes," I answer.

"Send me a friend request, and I'll keep you up to date on what's coming in the future," he adds.

"I will," I tell him, and with that we go our separate ways. I know I will be dreaming about this dance when my head hits that soft pillow tonight.

"So, you danced with Hector Ramos," Pablo teases me as I return. "What do you think? He's pretty good, huh?"

"Definitely, but not quite as good as you," I tease him back. "Okay, Pablo, I think I'm ready to call it a night."

"I would think so. They already announced the last dance before closing, but I don't think you noticed since you were talking to Hector," he laughs.

"Would you mind escorting me out?" I play with him by making a gesture towards the door.

"Yes," and adds, "and then I would like to take you somewhere to eat, if that's okay with you."

"Really?" I'm surprised. I hadn't thought about food, but just thinking the word makes me hungry.

"Yes, most of us go to a restaurant close by that's open twenty-four hours. You'll probably see quite a few of these people there, maybe even Hector," he laughs knowing I'm still star stunned.

"In that case," I reason, "how can I say no?"

Chapter 35 Scrambled Eggs with Pablo

I follow Pablo to a nearby Denny's restaurant. When we enter, I recognize a few people from the club, but no one I know well enough to say hello to. We find ourselves a booth and browse through the menu. It doesn't take long for a waitress to come for our orders.

"What can I get you?" Asks a lady in her mid-thirties wearing a name badge that reads "Josie".

"Scrambled eggs, wheat toast, and a coffee," I answer.

"That sounds good. I'll have the same," Pablo replies and smiles at the waitress as he hands her our menus. I watch her melt before my eyes. Who wouldn't?

"What do you think of LA?" Pablo asks me.

"I love it. I had so much fun. The dancers are amazing." As we talk, the waitress returns with our coffee. "Thank you," I tell her as she places mine on the table. I don't think she hears me, though. Her eyes never leave Pablo.

"I'm surprised you came alone. I thought Esteban would bring you."

"No, I asked him to take me, but he said I wasn't ready," I sip my coffee to keep myself calm.

"So, you came here without him. Does he know?" Pablo asks watching for my reaction.

"No. We broke up," I finally let the words out. He's the first person I've told.

"What happened?"

I consider not sharing the details, but then think otherwise. It's not good to keep this bottled up inside me. I need to get it out, and he's the safest person. He lives here in LA, far away from anyone else I know. If he tells Mike then it saves me from having to do it, and Mike wouldn't tell anyone back home.

So, I tell Pablo everything from our Grand Opening at the Grapevine to finding out about Esteban's trip to LA with Melinda to my quick exit. He listens without saying a word. He waits for me to get it all out.

"I saw them in El Tigre," he starts.

"You did?" I'm surprised, but I shouldn't be. Of course, Pablo lives in LA. He must go to El Tigre every week. Why wouldn't he have seen them?

"Esteban was hanging out with Luis Chavez. He did come with Melinda, and they did dance a lot. But honestly, Scarlet, they didn't look like a couple."

"Really? What makes you think that?"

"I'm a guy. I see how he looks at you, and how he looks at her. There's a big difference. To me, it looked more business-like. You know a student and teacher relationship. He wasn't holding her or sitting close to her," he pauses before beginning again, "and I was watching them pretty closely."

"You were?" I smile and can't help but laugh. He must have been trying to protect me. Esteban was right. The Salsa world is small and sees everything.

"Well, yes, for two reasons," he continues, "the first was for you. If I saw something going on I would have found a way to let you know. Secondly, watching you and Esteban together is like watching my own past from a distance."

"I don't understand." His words make no sense to me. I'm confused.

He laughs, "Oh Scarlet, you're not the only one here who has had the misfortune of falling in love with your Salsa teacher." His eyes focus on his coffee cup as if it were a crystal ball revealing something only to him.

"You too?" I laugh. It's one of those weak miserable laughs. You know the one where the only other choice is crying?

"Yes, unfortunately, me too," he sighs.

"How long ago?"

"It's been three years since we broke up," he looks out the window. I guess it's the only direction to look without having to see anyone else stare back.

"Do you still see her in the clubs?" I remember Cindy warning me what would happen if Esteban and I were to break up.

"Yes, in fact, she was there tonight."

"I'm sorry. It must be hard," I wonder if it still hurts him.

"Yes, but I manage."

"Did you introduce me to her?" I ask. I know it's a painful question, but curiosity gets the best of me. I regret it as soon as I hear it out loud.

"No, but I pointed her out to you," he answers and then guessing my next question adds,"it was Sonya."

"Sonya? She's a World Champion," the words come out as I think them. Luckily, he doesn't look hurt but laughs a little.

"Yeah, I have no idea why she chose me. She could have any guy she wanted, and when I met her I was just learning how to dance," he looks me in the eye as if to communicate that him and I are a lot alike.

"You remind me of myself back then, Scarlet," he tells me. "I just loved to dance. I had no idea why other than it made me feel good. I wanted so badly to learn and when I saw Sonya I was drawn to her. I don't know where I found the courage, but I asked her to dance. She's a sweet person so she said yes, and she said yes every time after that. I wonder sometimes if she offered to teach me just to save herself from having to endure such awful dances." I smile back at him. Thinking of our waitress's reaction to Pablo, I doubt that was Sonya's only reason.

"What was it like learning from her?" I ask.

"It was a lot of hard work. I felt dumb at times. The way she wanted me to move felt awkward, and she insisted that I count the beats out loud so I would learn faster. I felt like an idiot. Still, I wanted to learn so I practiced. Do you know what's worse than trying to follow a good dancer?" He asks me a question we both know the answer to, but I stay silent and let him say it. "Leading one, especially when she's a World Champion who happens to be so beautiful you can barely breathe."

I laugh, "You're right. That would be so much worse." Pablo really is my Salsa guardian angel. He knows exactly how I feel and that's why his words always bring comfort. I imagine him a few years back, eager to learn, wanting to impress her, and frustrated.

"What happened?" I ask.

"My ego got the better of me," he pauses before adding, "that and believing lies. In Salsa, everyone likes to talk. You can imagine the rumors flying about given Sonya was dancing at the clubs with me, her new boyfriend and a beginner. She was a champion and to compete she had to have a partner at her level which wasn't going to be me any time soon, if ever. After all, I'm not exactly young. Because she is a champion, all of the best dancers wanted to dance with her. It makes sense, right? To advertise her classes, she needs to show what she can do, and unfortunately, as a beginner I wasn't unable to lead her in those aerial stunts and jaw-dropping dips. So, I would stand by and watch, wishing it were me out there making her look amazing. And, I felt slighted when a good song would play and she'd ask me if she could dance with someone else. I should have understood, but the heart feels what it feels, and after a while I didn't want to feel hurt anymore."

I remain silent. I sense there is more to hear. I don't want to interrupt what's coming next.

"She tried to tell me it didn't matter. That she loved me, and loved dancing with me. It was just business and to be on top she had to have partners she could compete with. She wanted to build a life with me, and dancing was only one part of that," Pablo has a hard time with those last words, as if each syllable comes at a cost. "I kept listening to people. Especially friends who just wanted to look out for me, well-meaning I suppose, asking me to question whether she could really prefer me over those younger men who were obviously attracted to her. Friends who didn't want to see me get hurt. I think they were trying to protect me, but I should have thought more for myself. I should have listened to Sonya. I should have been willing to believe her when she said she loved me." He takes another long pause, "In the end, I broke up with her."

"How did she react?"

"She was hurt. She tried to get me to reconsider. Told me how much she loved me and didn't want to lose me. That what we had was special. But in the end when I wouldn't change my mind, she let me go. We never fought. It was just very sad," Pablo's speech slows to a crawl as he finishes.

"You're not over her, are you?" I state the obvious. I don't know why. Maybe just to bring it out in the open between us.

"No, but at least I thought I made the right decision. That is, until I watched your boyfriend with his student at El Tigre," Pablo replies. "It was like getting a glimpse into Sonya's world, seeing it from her perspective, which is much easier when your heart isn't on the line. For me, dancing is pure emotion. For Sonya and Esteban, it is also a business, something to succeed at. Love is separate. Love is what she had with me. I suspect Esteban feels the same way about you." Pablo's looks into my eyes. "It's not too late, Scarlet. Why don't you talk to him? See what he has to say?"

"I don't know. I don't understand why he would lie to me," I answer.

"I don't either. Maybe that is what you should ask him," he counters. "If you don't like his answer leave things the way they are, but you may not have the whole story. He told you that much himself."

"Mike doesn't like him for me. Mike's a guy, a smart guy. Maybe he sees something I don't?" I voice one of my fears.

"I don't know. Maybe he does. But Mike isn't dating Esteban, is he? Mike hasn't spent more than five minutes talking to him, has he? Why would you trust his judgement over your own?" Pablo asks.

"My friend Cindy was the one who spotted them in LA. She's a good friend too. I don't think she has any motive to hurt me. Why would she tell me unless she thought something was going on?" I hear my voice rise slightly not out of anger but confusion.

"I'm guessing she was worried something was going on and wanted you to find out more. She didn't see them do anything romantic, because that is not what I saw. So, find out more. Ask him." Pablo repeats himself. Every question I ask gets the same answer.

"I don't know If he will even talk to me," I voice my biggest fear.

"You don't know if you don't try," Pablo smiles. He sees he has won me over. I have no fight left. He's right. It's almost like hearing the ghost of myself speak through someone else's lips. I stay silent for a few minutes, staring at my coffee cup trying to see the future.

"Pablo, are you and Sonya still friends?" I ask.

"I like to think so, but we never talk. We say hello, but never much more than that. I don't even have the courage to ask her for a dance." His eyes can't hide the sadness.

"Maybe it's not too late," I throw the possibility out there to see if it will take root.

"I think too much time has passed. Don't wait too long, Scarlet. Talk to him." With those last words we gather our things and leave.

Pablo follows me to the hotel and watches from his car to make sure I get in safe.

I shower, change into my pajamas, and settle into bed. I glance at my phone for messages, double checking that none are from my boys. In one last moment of bravery, I send a friend request to Hector Ramos. I know I will never drive to LA for his lessons, but one can dream, right?

The pillow is heaven. I knew it would be. Instead of dreaming of my dance with Hector like I thought I would, I remember dancing with Esteban. I can still smell his cologne. I miss his voice on the phone asking me about my day.

Chapter 36 Dancing is Better Than a Bag of Chips

I'm headed towards Santa Barbara again. I know every twist and turn of the road between here and the Havana Night Club. The Salsa music calms me as I drive alone at night. I think about the last few days since my trip to LA. I've picked up the phone at least a dozen times to call Esteban, and not once have I actually dialed his number.

What is the point? I doubt he'd want to talk to me. I guess it doesn't matter. He lied to me. What answer could he give that could justify that? He knew how badly I wanted to go, and he took someone else. My gut tells me there is nothing going on between him and Melinda. If anything, he just loves dancing with her, and honestly, that alone is enough to make me feel miserable.

So, I am dragging myself to the Havana Night Club. If I stay home, I will drown my sorrows in a bowl of chocolate ice cream and probably follow it with a bag of chips. Besides, dancing is better than lying in bed wide awake wishing I could hear Esteban's voice.

Each day I go to work, but I am a shadow of myself. I doubt anyone can tell. I hide it well. I smile during my aerobics classes and listen to every Wellness client. I take care of my boys and clean the apartment. I practice Salsa every day. The only one who knows I'm just going through the motions is me. Here, out in the night by myself, I don't have to pretend. I feel the weight of the sadness. It lifted briefly in LA. I'm hoping tonight might give me another break. I'm sure it will return tomorrow, but if I can escape this loneliness for even a couple of hours the drive will be worth it.

I pull into the parking lot, and after doing one last makeup check, I head in. It's already eleven so the club will be crowded. I hear the music and it helps, but I'm not as excited as I normally would be. I'm dragging myself in out of sheer will, coaxing myself along, promising I will feel better if I just get inside. I don't notice him until I hear him call my name.

"Scarlet," I hear Esteban's voice and look up to see him standing in front of me.

"Esteban," I'm caught off guard and don't know what to say.

"Scarlet, can we talk?" He softens his voice like you would with a stray cat you're afraid will run away.

"Yes, I'd like that," I pause and consider my words carefully before adding, "I should have stayed and listened to you instead of leaving. I was upset. I'd like to hear what you have to say."

"I did try to call, many times," Esteban tells me keeping a soft tone to his voice to disarm any anger.

"I know. I wasn't ready to talk then," I figure now isn't the best time to tell him I changed my number.

"Scarlet, the reason I lied about going to LA was to hide a surprise I was working on for your birthday," Esteban shares and watches for my reaction. "I have something to show you. It's in my car. Will you come with me to see it?"

"Sure," I'm stunned, but I follow him anyways. He unlocks his car door and pulls out a flyer. He takes me under a nearby streetlight so I can see it. As I look at it, he explains it to me.

"I went to LA to ask Luis Chavez if he and his dance company would perform at your birthday party. I wanted to celebrate it at our next Salsa Night at the Grapevine. I wanted to surprise you by giving you this flyer. I was waiting for it to be finished. That's why I didn't tell you sooner. I'm sorry, Scarlet. I should have known someone might have seen me. Everyone in Salsa talks. I can only guess what you must have thought."

As he talks, I stare at the poster. It has a background with shades of red creating shapes of dancing couples. Luis and Sonya are dressed in black and posed in a deep back-bending dip. It's positioned so that Sonya is dipping straight towards you with her eyes looking outward as Luis towers above her with one hand supporting her abdomen, the other arm wrapped around her back, his intense gaze staring down at her. World Champions. The poster announces their performance at the Grapevine. My picture is right beneath theirs with my name in cursive letters, "Celebrating Scarlet's Birthday."

"Nobody's ever done anything like this for me before," I feel my eyes water. My husband never threw me a party. I can't even remember the last time he bought a birthday present.

"You deserve it. You've been working so hard. I know how much you wanted to see the dancers in LA, so I thought I'd bring the best dancers here to celebrate your birthday." I'm quiet for a moment as I let the words sink in. When I speak, I voice the one thing I still do not understand.

"Esteban, can I ask you something?" I ask.

"Sure," he answers.

"Why did you take Melinda with you?"

"I haven't seen Luis for a couple of years. The dancers in LA are really good. I didn't want to show up after all this time and look like I couldn't dance. I took Melinda because she knows my combinations. Luis still intimidates me. He makes me nervous. He's my teacher. I wanted to dance at my best." He watches for my reaction. When I stay silent, he continues on.

"I guess I'm hard on you, because Luis was tough on me. He knew I really wanted to learn how to dance, and so he pushed me to get better. You remind me of myself, Scarlet. I'm harder on you than the others, because I want you to be one of the best dancers. I

207

know you want to learn as much as I did. I see how much you practice to try and impress me. That's how I feel with Luis, and that's the only reason I took Melinda with me. I promise you. I didn't do anything with Melinda. I would never cheat on you with her or anyone else," Esteban looks me in the eye and doesn't look away. I believe him.

"I'm sorry, Esteban. I should have listened. I shouldn't have doubted you."

"Scarlet, you never talk about your divorce. I'm guessing it involved your husband lying to you," he says the words careful and slow, as if it would lessen the sting. I can't speak. I hand him back the flyer and wipe the tears that have slipped out from my eyes. He takes the flyer and with his free arm he draws me near. The smell of the cologne I've missed. He comes close to kiss me, and I meet him halfway.

It's a sweet kiss, full of unspoken apologies.

"Promise me you won't run away again. Next time, we talk, okay?" He tells me as we pull a part.

"I promise."

"Scarlet, can I take you out for coffee tonight? I know you love to dance, but I miss talking to you. Would you mind?" He asks.

"I'd love to," I answer. As much as I love to dance, I don't think anything could make me happier tonight than sitting next to Esteban, listening to him share about his day, his dreams, what he hopes will happen next, and hearing the question I've been missing most of all, "Scarlet, how was your day?"

Chapter 37 It's My Birthday

This is the most beautiful dress I've ever owned. Tonight, we celebrate my birthday at the Grapevine. I twirl around in front of the mirror watching how the dress moves with me. The fabric is better quality than any I've ever put on my body. The color makes it stand out. I have other red dresses, but this is more vibrant than any other red I've worn before. It's a simple dress with spaghetti straps that bare my shoulders and a short hemline to highlight my legs. Elegant in its simplicity. I feel extra beautiful wearing it, because I remember the day Esteban bought it for me.

Two weeks ago, he asked me to meet him in Santa Barbara to help him shop for clothes for our big event. We spent an entire Saturday afternoon visiting shop after shop looking for an outfit for him. It took forever to finally decide on the right one. As we walked back to our cars, he stopped at one last place, an expensive looking store that I normally would pass on by. He picked up a sleeveless black dress with a low cut back and a tiny white dress with silver fringes. He asked me if I saw anything that I liked. I was drawn to this red dress.

He had me try on the dresses. I modeled them for him thinking it was just for fun. Afterwards, he took the dresses to the front counter and bought all three, my birthday present.

I can't count how many posters I've put up announcing my birthday. My face along with two World Champions plastered in numerous spots throughout Lompoc, Santa Ynez, Solvang, Buellton, Santa Barbara and maybe even in Oxnard if I know Esteban. I've been dutifully posting it on social media every few days for three weeks now. I've told all my friends and most are coming out for it. My poor boys have heard me talk about it every day. They smile and listen, but I'm guessing inside they must think they have the weirdest mom ever. With these thoughts roaming through my head, I gather my things and make the drive to the Grapevine.

When I drive into the parking lot, I see that Esteban's caravan has already arrived. Inside the Grapevine, I find Esteban, Fernando, Marco, and Marisol hanging out by the stage. I say hello and give a round of hugs.

Esteban pulls me close to him for a hug and kiss, "Happy Birthday, Scarlet. Are you excited about tonight?"

"Yes, I can't believe this is really happening. I get to see Luis and his company perform. And this dress is so beautiful! I can't believe you did this for me," I try to keep the emotion down in my voice, but it's impossible to hide.

"You deserve it, and you look beautiful. I've got to talk to the deejay and go over some last minute details. I don't want you to worry about anything. I just want to enjoy tonight, okay?" Before walking away, he kisses me one more time and holds me close. What more could I want for my birthday?

People should be arriving soon, and shortly after Luis Chavez will teach the Salsa lesson. I can't wait. I get to take a lesson by a ten-time World Champion on my birthday. My LA dream come true.

Angie is the first of my friends to arrive. Gone are the black yoga pants and sweatshirt I see her in every day. Tonight she's wearing a sleeveless blue silk top with blue jeans and high heels. Her short blonde hair is perfect for showing off her shiny hoop earrings.

"I can't believe you're here!" I tell her as I give her a hug. "You look beautiful!"

"Thanks. Look at you! That dress is to die for. Okay, point him out. Which one is Esteban?" Angie wastes no time getting down to business. I laugh as I nod in his direction.

"He's the one with a serious face talking to the deejay," as I single him out Angie looks him over carefully.

"Can I have one too, please? I think I want to take Salsa lessons. Do all the instructors look like him?" Angie teases, but I know she would never leave her husband, not for a thousand gorgeous men. Her husband adores her, and she lights up whenever she talks about him, even if she's complaining.

More and more friends come through the door and I do my best to greet them all. Gym members, clients, students, co-workers, neighbors, dancers from Santa Barbara, and even Tina, the gossipy front desk person, they are all here. The divorce may have severed my little family in two, but watching people enter the Grapevine I realize that I've made so many friends since then. I hear a familiar voice behind me.

"There she is the Amazing Birthday girl," I turn around to see not only Mike, but Pablo and a woman standing behind me. Looking closer, I see a resemblance. She has Pablo's hair color and a similarity in the shape of her eyebrows. The eye color is different. Hers is a brilliant green that draws you in. She's neither heavy nor slender, but somewhere in between. We look about the same age. I'm guessing she's Pablo's younger sister. She's wearing a silky black dress with black heels and a sweet smile.

"Scarlet, I'd like you to meet my sister, Lupe," Pablo takes charge of the introductions.

"Happy birthday! I'm so glad I get to finally meet you!" Lupe surprises me with a bear hug. "I've heard all about you from these two. I feel like I know you already."

"I'm so happy to meet you too. Mike told me you've been helping him learn how to dance," I say as I hug her back. She still hasn't let me go. I like her already.

"Yes," Lupe looks a little shy as she pulls away and glances in Mike's direction. I read Mike's expression. He likes her. I wonder if he's told her yet. Nothing would make me happier than to see him with a girl like her. Of course, his boot camp class might go into a serious depression and chug gallons of chocolate ice cream for a week, but they'll work it off.

"Do me a favor and keep him out on the dance floor all night," I tell her as I smile and look in Mike's direction. I can see how happy he is when he looks at her. I have a good feeling about them.

I see more people piling in. Anticipation floats about the air as we wait for the Champions. When the time for the lesson comes and goes without their arrival, I start to worry. I also notice that Esteban is missing. I check with Fernando, and he tells me that the pair got lost trying to find the Grapevine. Esteban has gone to find them and bring them here. The deejay makes a short announcement informing the crowd of the delay and then invites everyone to the dance floor.

I notice dancers I've never seen before, and they're really good. I wonder if they're part of Luis's dance team. I haven't had the guts to ask. Instead, I just watch them from the sidelines.

Through the crowd, I see Cindy walk through the doors. She has her long straight hair let loose and flowing down to her waist, a black top with bare shoulders and short sleeves, skin-tight black pants, and red heels added for a splash of color. Several men watch her as she passes them by.

"I haven't seen you since we last talked. I've been so worried," Cindy shares as she gives me a hug.

"I went through a rough time, but it all worked out," I reassure her as I hug her back.

"I can see that. I'm glad everything turned out all right for you. Luis Chavez performing for your birthday bash. I'm so excited for

212

you!" Cindy says as she looks around the room taking in the growing crowd.

"I feel spoiled rotten, but I'm loving it. I can't believe Esteban did this for me." I pause before adding, "It means a lot to me that you're here." As I say the words out loud I can feel how true they are to me. Friends like Cindy and Mike are hard to find. I imagine she must have worried that I would be angry with her, especially since Esteban and I are still together. She came anyways. Mike and Cindy may not always be right, but they love me enough to tell the truth just the way they see it.

As I look around the room, I notice heads turning towards the doorway. Luis and Sonya enter and follow Esteban to the stage. Luis grabs a microphone from the deejay and speaks to the crowd.

"Sorry, I'm late. I got lost, but let's get this started. Let's get you moving to warm up, and then I'll break down the steps," as Luis hands the microphone back to the deejay, the music begins. I can feel the excitement course through the crowd as we begin to move with him.

Luis faces us as he dances on stage, smiling down at us trying to follow him. He uses his hands to point us in the right direction and to signal changes in the steps. His clothes are simple, not what you would expect from a World Champion. He has a black polo shirt and jeans paired with black and white dance shoes. He could be wearing a potato sack. The way he moves makes his clothes irrelevant. He is more graceful and polished than any dancer I've seen before.

Sonya is in front of us on the dance floor. She has her back to us. We follow her so we don't get lost when Luis changes directions. Her clothes are simple too. She's wearing an off the shoulder grey sweater paired with a long skirt with a slit down one side. Her blonde hair is pulled back into a long ponytail. Her posture is perfect and her movements elegant. I can imagine the pangs of loss

Pablo must have to endure watching her. I try my best not to look in his direction. I'm afraid I'll see heartache in his eyes.

I'm standing in the back. I don't know why. I guess I want to see everything. From Luis on stage smiling down on us to the reaction of the dancers below following him. There has to be over fifty dancers on the floor.

Luis's steps are handpicked for beginners. I'm sure Esteban told him most people in this area have little experience dancing Salsa. I already know these steps, but Luis adds subtle changes to them. As he breaks them down, he offers details that make his steps stand out from others. When he does the Cumbia step he doesn't let the torso turn from side to side. He only allows the bottom half of his body to pivot right and left as he does the rock step to the back. His top half stays forward. He also adds an extra tap before beginning the rock step. Each of these changes makes the movement look polished. As he introduces each step, he adds these special touches. I can see why he is the best in the world ten times over.

After teaching us footwork for an hour, Luis tells us to grab a partner. A young man, probably in his twenties, offers me his hand and we find a spot on the floor. Chances are he's part of the dance team, because I haven't seen him in Santa Barbara or Oxnard. Luis and Sonya are in the middle. The rest of the couples are arranged in a giant circle around them.

The World Champions demonstrate the moves and us regular folk try our best to copy them. Luis does all of the talking, breaking down steps and giving pointers, but my attention rests on Sonya.

She has something in the way she moves that I want for myself. Even with Luis explaining her movements, and then watching her demonstrate them over and over, none of us can match her moves exactly. She has finishing touches that make her look better than the rest of us. It reminds me of a master chef that shares most of the ingredients in a recipe, but holds back a few special ones so that his dish still tastes the best. I watch her closely trying to steal a few of her secrets. How does she glide across the floor? Why can't I seem to mimic her good posture even when I'm standing as tall as I can? As I survey the other female dancers around me, I see they have no idea how she does it either.

When the lesson comes to an end, the deejay cues the music and opens the dance floor. Luis and Sonya are surrounded by fans who want to take a picture with them.

"Don't you want to take a picture?" Esteban asks as he puts his arm around me. I lean my head on his shoulder.

"No, I already have a poster of the three of us which I have framed and hanging on my bedroom wall," I answer as I snuggle in closer to him.

"Are you happy?" He asks.

"Very," I reply.

"Are you sure I can't convince you to do the birthday dance?" Esteban tries one more time to change my mind.

This is a question he has been asking me since the first night he told me about this Salsa birthday party. The birthday dance is a tradition in the Salsa club. The dancers form a circle around the birthday boy or girl and each take a turn dancing with them while the birthday song plays. I've told Esteban repeatedly there's no way I'm doing it with a ten-time World Champion and his team of dancers in my line up. The fear in my eyes convinces Esteban once again that I am serious.

"I'm not doing it, and I'll never forgive you if you surprise me with it."

"I won't," he laughs. He takes my hand and spins me out onto the dance floor.

This is the first time I've seen him relaxed and playful since we started planning for this event. I guess seeing the successful turn out has lifted a weight off his shoulders. He keeps me moving with his seventy plus combinations, each flowing seamlessly into the next. I can follow him easily now. I know the feel of his hands and react without thinking. I can't remember when I crossed over the line of being clueless and stressed to following without thought. It must have happened at some point after hours and hours of practice when I was too tired to notice, but it feels incredible tonight. We dance three songs back to back completely in sync with each other.

He takes me into a triple spin, something we've done countless times before, and I stop perfectly in front of him. Just in time to see Luis' face as he walks by us. He gives a double take, smiles and nods at Esteban. It's that look of pride that only a teacher has and there is no mistaking it. Esteban is shocked by the recognition. He smiles and laughs it off, but I can see it has an effect on him. After that his ability to lead deteriorates. It's almost comical. He's undone and impossible to follow. Instead of being frustrated, we laugh at our misfortune.

"I couldn't follow you. After Luis walked by that was it," I tease him when the song comes to an end.

"I know. Luis makes me nervous," Esteban confesses.

"That's okay. I know the feeling," I sympathize with him. I kiss his cheek and let him make his rounds about the venue.

It's actually a nice birthday present. It shows me that we're all vulnerable when we are learning. Seeing him like this will remind me not to be so hard on myself in the future. What does it really matter anyways? Dance horrible one song and beautiful the next. It's all the same if you enjoy every moment. The ocean and life itself share this cycle too. We ride life's ocean wave from the peak of the summit to the crash on the shoreline and when we think it's all over the big wide ocean pulls us back in to begin again. The secret to surviving the despair of the crash is to remember it is all part of the same ride, and just as music guides the dancer, the ocean guides the wave, there is something out there guiding us along.

I take turns dancing with Mike, Pablo, Fernando, Marco, men I know from Santa Barbara, and even the LA dancers. I collect birthday wishes with each dance.

Luis and Sonya dance together for most of the songs, while the rest of us watch awe struck. Each one is mesmerizing on their own, but together they do moves that are hypnotic. Sonya's flexibility is unnatural. Luis can spin so many times on his own that I get dizzy watching him. How do they move like that? The crowd wonders. And yet, the pair go on song after song like it is nothing out of the ordinary. Effortless.

I head outside for fresh air. The exterior of the Grapevine looks like a big wooden barn with its two front doors wide open so you can see the dancing inside. I stare at the starry sky overhead. The same one I've watched many times at the Havana Night Club. The feeling never changes. Gratitude. I am so grateful to be here doing what I love.

"So you finally took a break," I hear Esteban's voice off to my right. "I have someone I want you to meet."

I turn towards Esteban and see Luis standing next to him.

"Hi," I manage to say as Luis holds out his hand to greet me.

"I've heard a lot about you from this guy," Luis tells me as he shakes my hand.

I'm too star struck to say anything clever, or really, anything at all. Instead, I reflexively smile and then avoid his eyes. Sensing my embarrassment, Luis continues on, "This guy and I go way back. He's a good friend. I'd do anything for him."

217

"Nah," Esteban gets embarrassed and looks downward too.

"Yeah, I think he's very special. One of a kind," I find my voice long enough to agree with Luis. He smiles back in return.

"I guess it's time for us to perform," Luis turns to Esteban and then motions to the open door.

"Yes," Esteban recovers and starts to lead him inside. Luis turns back to me one last time.

"I'm glad I got to meet you, Scarlet. Take good care of this guy for me, okay?"

"I will," I promise. I watch them head towards the stage. I follow shortly behind and stand towards the back of the room taking the entire scene in. I want to store it in my memory forever. The colors, the sound of the music, dresses spinning on the dance floor, men twirling the ladies, and Esteban taking the stage to announce the upcoming performance. This is the best birthday present I've been given. I don't expect there will ever be one better.

The dance company is scheduled to perform two numbers. The first being a Salsa danced by Luis and Sonya, the same routine that won them the World Championship title. The crowd cheers as the pair walk on to the dance floor.

Sonya stands in the center of the floor wearing a sheer pink dress of satin and rhinestones, and Luis dressed all in black comes up behind and embraces her. The music begins as he unwraps her away from him, only to pull her towards him again into a wild ride of combinations. The footwork is intricate and quick as lightening, but that doesn't stop the pair from playing with the crowd with eye contact and facial expressions. Sonya lifts her leg so high in the air I'm surprised it doesn't hit her head. Luis whips her around his body like she weighs nothing. As the song comes to a close, Luis throws her into the air and she arches her back at the peak of the toss only to collapse in on herself as he catches her in his arms. He carries her as he spins them both before lowering her to the ground in front of him with his arms still wrapped around her. They end as they began. The Grapevine explodes with clapping and whistles.

Sonya exits the floor while Luis remains. He is joined by the rest of the dance team. The men are dressed to match Luis. The ladies are in short black dresses with long sleeves and V-necklines outlined in rhinestones. Everyone has a black hat. One of the female dancers carries Luis' hat out to him, and when she places it on his head the music starts. The team moves as one. Even the revolutions of the ladies' spins are timed perfectly with one another. How this is accomplished at top speed is beyond me. None of them match Luis' command of the footwork, but a couple of the male dancers come close. As the music builds to the finish, the entire team stops in a straight line facing forward to the crowd. Then cued by the song, one dancer turns his hard sharply to the right followed by the next and so on creating a domino effect. When the last dancer turns their head, the guys grab the hand of the woman next to him and pulls her into a fast double spin catching her and dipping her low. The audience erupts with cheers. People clap and whistle. I hear at least a dozen yelling, "Encore!"

The performance done, the deejay opens the floor again for dancing. People are reluctant to dance. I'm guessing they're intimidated. Whatever we're capable of seems a lifetime away from what we just witnessed. Nobody wants to be the first to venture out there. For the first couple of minutes, the dance floor remains empty.

"Would you like to dance?" I hear Pablo's voice next to me and then see his outstretched hand.

"Always," I answer as I place my hand in his.

"Are you enjoying your birthday?" He asks.

"Yes, I can't believe it. I'll never have another birthday like it."

"That's probably true," he laughs. "I don't think Esteban can top this one. I'm glad things worked out for you two."

"Your advice helped a lot."

"So, I guess his trip to LA was all about arranging this party, huh?" Pablo says as he takes us to the center of the floor. We're the only couple out here.

"Yes," I answer.

"Well, I'm glad. This is a great party," he tells me as he gives a goofy grin and starts me moving.

I give him just the weight of my hands as he taught me. I become a blank slate. He gives me that smile that lets me know this is going to be pure fun and nothing else. There is no more worry. Right and wrong doesn't exist. Perfection is not what we are here for. We are here only to enjoy the dance.

Little by little, others join us on the floor. Maybe it's easier for them to give it a try seeing two normal people just having fun. No aerial stunts required. I can't help but laugh seeing how many different ways Pablo can surprise me. He dances on the fine line between masterful and comical. He's an amazing dancer who refuses to take it too seriously. In the periphery of my vision, I notice Sonya watching us. Watching me? It's hard to get a good look and follow Pablo's lead, but I know I'm right. Her face doesn't look angry or jealous, but she isn't smiling either. I'm not sure if Pablo notices. I think of asking him, but the song ends before I get the chance.

"Thank you," I tell him as I give him a hug.

"Happy birthday, Scarlet," he gives me one last birthday wish as he turns to walk away.

"Can I have this dance?" I hear a voice behind me and when I turn around I see Luis standing there.

Chapter 38 Dancing with the Champions

I reluctantly place my hand in his. I'm trying to think up some kind of excuse, while he drags me over to dance in front of the stage. I think he senses my deep desire to say no and is not giving me the opportunity. Most of his dance team is seated on the edge of the stage. This has been their hang out for most of the evening. I'm scared. His dance team is watching us. I'm on the verge of making a break and running.

I feel a calm wash over me. The ghost of myself speaks up.

"When will you ever dance with a World Champion again? Who cares who is watching? Did you ever think you would do this?" Her voice whispers into my ear, "It's a gift. When this is gone, it will be gone forever, so live it to the fullest."

Her words are like a magical spell that brings me back to myself. I know I will hold on to her words long after this dance. She's not just talking about dancing, but life itself. When it's gone, it's gone forever, so don't take it for granted. Enjoy.

He starts out easy with a few basics and a right-hand turn, but when he signals me to walk across him with a double spin I get slightly off-balanced. It startles me.

"Keep your eyes on me," Luis instructs as he points two fingers at his own eyes. His tone isn't strict or frustrated, but informative like a helpful hint. His words have an immediate effect. My attention is laser-focused. I use his head as a point of reference for every spin, twist and turn. My ability to follow increases exponentially. It becomes effortless. I think part of the ease has to do with being Esteban's teacher. He leads like Esteban. I feel less scared. I know I can read his signals. As if he can sense my confidence, he starts bringing on the combinations and the speed. It is the roller coaster ride I hope for in every dance.

I know I will never remember what moves we did together. I won't even remember how Luis danced. What I will never forget was how it felt to be in the moment. To put aside my fear and embrace life. Gratitude for its surprises, and humility for its surprises. Yes, bad things come out of nowhere, but then again, good things come from there as well. I'm not always in control. I live in an upside down world where the unexpected can happen. Thank God the unexpected can happen.

I notice Luis give a quick glance to Esteban and smile. He's telling him something I'm sure, but I can't figure out what it might be. Esteban smiles back and laughs a little.

As the song comes to an end, Luis gives me a hug.

"Happy birthday, Scarlet," he tells me.

"Thank you for coming and bringing your team. You don't know how much this has meant to me."

"You're welcome," he answers. With those parting words, I head over to Esteban.

"Did you see? I danced with Luis. I was scared to death. Did I do okay?" I ask Esteban.

"Yes," Esteban smiles as he pulls me close to him.

"Thank you for everything. This is the best birthday I've ever had. I think this will be the best birthday of my entire life," I tell him as I give him a kiss on his cheek. He laughs and looks away embarrassed at my sentiment.

"Why did Luis look at you while we were dancing?" I ask.

"That's because he was going crazy. Everyone was watching because Luis was doing some incredible footwork while he was dancing with you," Esteban lets me in on what everyone else saw.

"I didn't notice. I was too busy trying to follow his lead. I messed up on the first double spin and he told me to watch him. So, that's what I did the whole time, I didn't take my eyes off his head." I can't help but laugh. "I guess I missed it." Esteban puts his arm around my shoulders and I lean into him. It doesn't matter one bit if I missed what others saw. I danced with a ten-time World Champion on my birthday. I would have never imagined this the first night I got in my car and drove to Santa Barbara by myself. As many times as I daydreamed during those long drives to the Havana Night Club, I never came close to imagining something this wonderful.

"Scarlet, do you have any idea how beautiful you are? I couldn't keep my eyes off of you," Esteban tells me softly as I let my body nestle into him.

"Thank you, Esteban. Thank you for everything," I answer. I feel beautiful. The kind of beauty that comes from deep inside and puts a smile on your face.

We see a group of people start to leave. Esteban heads over to say goodbye and to thank them for coming. I see Sonya walk towards me. I'm not sure why. Maybe she's going to wish me a happy birthday.

"Hi, I haven't had a chance to say hello. Happy Birthday!" She tells me as she gives me a hug. The introduction seems a little forced and awkward, but I'm excited to finally speak to her. She's been dancing all night, and yet she smells incredible. World Champion dancer uses first class perfume. Makes sense. It is so much better than what I smell like.

"Thank you, and thank you for coming tonight and performing. You and the entire team made my birthday! You were absolutely beautiful out there."

"You're welcome," she smiles and then stands beside me while we watch the dancers. There aren't many left. Most are heading home. The night is almost done. She turns towards me again.

"Where have you and Luis danced before?" She asks.

"We haven't," I answer. "This was my first time dancing with him, and I was scared to death!" I laugh after hearing myself out loud. Such drama for a grown woman, but yeah, I was terrified.

"Huh," she pauses before continuing, "it looked like you guys had danced before."

"Wow, no, this was the first time I've ever met him," I answer. We keep watching the dancers. She doesn't walk away.

"I'm surprised you're not out there dancing. I imagine every guy in the club wants to dance with you," I try to come up with something to talk about.

"I don't think the guys here want to ask me. I might be intimidating for some of them," she answers as though this is not an uncommon problem. Of course, that makes sense. I recall Pablo telling me how she made him nervous when he was learning.

"Too bad. This is a good song," she says quietly.

"Maybe you should ask one?" I tease.

"Do you think so?"

"Yes."

"Do you know one who is a good dancer?" She asks.

"Yes, I do," I pause for a moment before revealing him. Am I sure I want to do this? I remember Sonya's face as she watched us dance together. I understand why she is talking to me now. I follow my hunch. "That guy over there with the sandy blonde hair. He is very handsome, yes? His name is Pablo, and he is my friend. I'm really worried about him. I know dancing with you would cheer him up."

"Worried? Is he sick?" Sonya blurts out the question. Fear. Panic. It's all in her voice. She looks pale like she's forgotten how to breathe.

"No, he's not sick. He's sad. It's about a girl," I regret the words as soon as they come out. I see Sonya's body stiffen. Quickly I add, "A woman he was deeply in love with three years ago. She was his dance teacher. He's never gotten over her. He told me losing her was the biggest mistake of his life. Pablo said he would never find another woman like her." After hearing my words, Sonya's face softens.

"Why did he let her go?" She asks.

"He didn't believe a woman as special as her could really love him. He's learned a lot since then, and understands where he was wrong." I try to pick the right words. Searching through my memories from our breakfast together. Recalling everything he told me. Hoping that by giving her his words they might work magic. "He knows he hurt her badly. He doesn't even have the courage to ask her for a dance, even though he has wanted to many times."

"Do you really think if I ask him to dance that would make him happy?" Sonya questions as she looks directly at me. My guess is she is looking for my reaction. She wonders if I know that the girl is really her. She is testing the waters. I choose my reply carefully.

"I know it would. Pablo has told me what a sweet person you are, Sonya. I imagine he would want you to do whatever makes you happy. I know that happiness is what he wants most for you." With that last bit, I have stuck my neck out on the chopping block. Here, I meet a World Champion, and I am trying to play matchmaker. She could be hating me right now.

Sonya keeps quiet for a while as she watches the dancers. Then she smiles at me.

"Thank you," she says softly before she leaves. I watch her walk towards Pablo.

I can't help but laugh watching Pablo's face as he figures out she is walking towards him. I see him check to his right and left just to make sure he's not mistaken. His whole face lights up when he realizes she is coming for him. She extends her hand to him, and he takes it. Gently, he guides her to a spot on the dance floor, far away from any other couple, as if she is a porcelain doll that might easily break if bumped by other dancers.

The deejay is playing one of my favorites. It's a happy tune that penetrates down to the soul and makes you want to dance forever.

Instead of being nervous, Pablo flashes her his goofy grin. The one that says that with him everything will be all right. This will be fun no matter what happens. He spins her in towards him, and I watch a World Champion melt in his arms. The next moment he has her moving all around him. The two of them laughing as much as they are dancing. It doesn't matter who might spin Sonya in all kinds of contorted positions, toss her high in the air, or help her win her next championship. No man will make her face light up like Pablo.

"Do you have enough energy left to dance with me?" Esteban asks. I've been so taken with Sonya and Pablo I didn't see Esteban sneak up on me.

"Always," I answer as I take his hand. The roller coaster ride I love. He spins me on to the floor and rushes into join me. The last song of the night and I can feel he is going to give me what I want. Pushing my limits of what I think I am capable of. Can I keep up with him? What will he do next? Challenging me and surprising me like only he can. This is what I look for in every dance, and with him I always find it.

Sonya and Pablo. Scarlet and Esteban. People can drift apart and find their way back again. Others drift away and are carried by the current to someone new. A new start, a new love, a new life. It doesn't matter really. It's all part of the same dance. The music plays for all of us. We each come to it in our own way. Cindy and the Bachelors of the Havana Night Club live only for the carnival. Esteban and Luis are driven like a relentless drum to be the best. To Pablo, music is the language of love. As for Sonya, she dances between the two worlds of perfection and passion, keeping them both separate but close.

For me, the music calls me out into the night, following the whispers and invitations to another life waiting for me. It culls the parts of me that don't belong. It gives me the courage to start the car and begin the journey. Following hunches and clues to find what I lost long ago, myself.

And somewhere, watching always watching, the ghost of myself is happy. I've learned to follow her lead. Her signals are easy to read now. Forever haunting me to go beyond what I think is possible. She is what I search for in every dance. And in the music, I can hear her laughter as she tells me, "How I love you! I can't believe how much you've grown. But sweetheart, you still have a long way to go before you dance like me!"

A Special Thank You

I want to thank my family and friends who have shared my journey. My boys who are and who will always be my greatest gift in life. My parents who are two pillars of strength and love. I'd like to thank Elizabeth Morgan for being my first reader and biggest cheerleader. Judy Scher and Mary Ann Weyandt for providing invaluable feedback and support.

A special heartfelt thank you to every dancer I've encountered in the past ten years and to the Salsa community in the 805 area. The dance teachers who have graciously given their time and talent to make me a better dancer. And last, but never least, Efrain Estrada who taught me to dance Salsa and remains my partner in dance and life.

About the Author

Who am I? Hmm, let me see if I can capture this in one ghastly paragraph. During the day, I toil at a Junkyard with smelly men. At night, I crave the dance floor. In the wee morning hours, I sip my coffee and try to capture the magic I see floating about in everyday life. I dance with fact and fiction, and write the stories I find that live in the in-between.

I also have a Bachelor Degree in Developmental Psychology from Eastern Washington University, which explains my lifelong passion of trying to understand why people do weird things.

I worked as a Personal Trainer for four years and loved every moment. If you are just starting a workout routine, let me be the first one to tell you that you can do it!

I still take dance lessons and try to venture onto the dance floor at least once a week. I haven't found anything else yet (except for writing) that makes me feel so alive.

I know what it is like to struggle through a divorce and my heart goes out to anyone in the middle of healing from one. I hope that you will find some comfort in my story, as you begin to write a new one for yourself.

This is my first book, but I am already working on the next. Please subscribe to raeshellrozet.blog and like my Facebook fan page, Raeshell Rozet, the Dancing Writer, to find more of my short stories.

As I said in the beginning, I hope my writing encourages you to follow your own curiosities. Thank you for reading.

Made in the USA
San Bernardino, CA
23 January 2020

63408008R00146